Confessions of a Teenage Baboon

> "I'm just going to tell you the story the way it happened, and I'm afraid it's going to shock a few people. Most of what I'm going to confess has to do with when I was fifteen years old. But I'm sixteen now, so I'm not as demented as I was then . . ."
>
> —Chris Boyd

"Zindel's magic makes his new novel an experience so real that events are heard and felt rather than read . . . The book is deftly constructed and moving as well as funny."

—*Publishers Weekly*

"Zindel has a caustic comic touch . . . and a talent for spotlighting bizarre and dramatic scenes."

—*Kirkus Reviews*

Paul Zindel

Confessions of a Teenage Baboon

BANTAM BOOKS
TORONTO · NEW YORK · LONDON

This low-priced Bantam Book
has been completely reset in a type face
designed for easy reading, and was printed
from new plates. It contains the complete
text of the original hard-cover edition.
NOT ONE WORD HAS BEEN OMITTED.

CONFESSIONS OF A TEENAGE BABOON
*A Bantam Book | publishd by arrangement with
Harper & Row, Publishers, Inc.*

PRINTING HISTORY
Harper & Row edition published October 1977
Bantam edition | October 1978
2nd printing
3rd printing
4th printing

ISBN 0-553-11829-3

Published simultaneously in the United States and Canada

Bantam Books are published by Bantam Books, Inc. Its trade-
mark, consisting of the words "Bantam Books" and the por-
trayal of a bantam, is registered in the United States Patent
Office and in other countries. Marca Registrada. Bantam
Books, Inc., 666 Fifth Avenue, New York, New York 10019.

PRINTED IN THE UNITED STATES OF AMERICA

To Bonnie

1

I'M JUST GOING TO TELL YOU THE STORY THE WAY IT HAP-
pened, and I'm afraid it's going to shock a few people.
Most of what I'm going to confess has to do with when
I was fifteen years old. But I'm sixteen now, so I'm
not as demented as I was then.

First of all, you've got to know that I'm from Staten
Island, which is a piece of land surrounded by water
just south of the Statue of Liberty. It's sort of a geo-
graphical version of a detached retina. And we really
like each other on Staten Island although once in a
while some of the folks borrow car parts from each
other without asking, and there's a little breaking and
entering that goes on. Also, ten years ago a seven-
year-old girl knocked off her parents with a kitchen
knife while they were sleeping, but that was an ex-
ception. We also have a zoo with the only albino
python on the eastern seacoast, and any day you want

you can go at three o'clock in the afternoon and watch them feed it the most expensive, succulent, toxified rats.

What I'm going to confess to you here is so mindboggling that it may haunt you the rest of your life. This is a warning to any kids with a heart condition. My story has a lot of torment, fights, and at least one good car crash. In fact, if they make this book into a movie, that's what I want to call it: *Torment, Fights, and at Least One Good Car Crash.* But to be more specific, my story has terrible things in it, and I want to tell you straight off they're all true. It also has my mother in it, and she's what's known as a small-time shoplifter. She doesn't steal diamonds or payrolls or knock off banks. She takes little things like cans of Campbell's Chicken Noodle soup, postage stamps, and jars of chunky peanut butter. Then there's this other important character in the book by the name of Lloyd Dipardi who's a drunken shipyard worker, and he does things that get him into a lot of trouble. And there are some cops in this story who do some very violent things because they can get away with it on Staten Island, particularly in the hick town of Oakwood Kills where my story takes place. The last thing I've got to tell you is there are things that are done to me in this story that aren't very nice—but I'm going to tell you anyway because maybe some of you will learn something from them. Maybe there are some of you who are as ashamed and mixed up as I was and don't know how to handle the problems of being alive that people don't warn you about. And that's the main reason I'm writing this confession—because I don't think

2

we should go on keeping quiet about these things. All the lying has to stop somewhere. The only thing that's going on in my mind is that I hope when you finish reading this you won't hate me. Please don't despise me for being the one to tell you that the days of being Huckleberry Finn are gone forever.

2

THE WHOLE CATASTROPHE HAPPENED BECAUSE MY MOTH-
er, whom I always refer to as Helen, is a practical
nurse and she and I went to live in Lloyd Dipardi's
house last July. We did that because Lloyd Dipardi
hired Helen to take care of his mother, Mrs. Carmelita Dipardi, who was coming home from the hospital
to live out her illness with her family.

We were very lucky my mother got the job because
at that time we had no place to live. My mother didn't
just take care of the very ill. Sometimes she was someone's companion. But the job I liked her to have best
was taking care of newborn babies. Aside from the
fact that she was always too tired from all those night
feedings to keep pestering me, I always felt renewed
to see a little tot enter the world. It always filled me
with great hope to think that maybe this little person
could be someone terrific if he was given a chance.

Between jobs my mother and I usually lived at the Ritz Hotel which is the kind of hotel where you have to step over derelicts in order to make it through the lobby. Anyway, my mother's full name is Helen Boyd. And my name is Christopher. My friends would call me Chris, but I didn't have any friends. No *real* friends. I also have no father. Now, once upon a time I did have a father, and my father and Helen really loved each other very much for the first seven years they were married, and then after that they hated each other so much that my father pulled that old trick of saying he was going out to buy the evening paper but went to Mexico. As far as I know he lived for about three months in Guadalajara and then Helen received the news that he died from an overdose of amoebas. That's one of the first things I learned about Life; it's not always like you read about in your local newspaper. It's more like what you read in the *National Enquirer.* So the first important thing I've confessed to you is that since I was five years old I was raised without a father. I have only a few memories of him like he loved animals and took me to the zoo and he liked dogs and he told me to eat the beets on my plate because they were good for me. I also remember he was bigger than me and I was really impressed by that. One day long after he had left, I saw a chesterfield overcoat in one of our closets and I asked Helen whose it was and she said it had belonged to my father. Now I realize a chesterfield overcoat is not much of a legacy, but I adopted the coat and I always took the coat with me no matter where we moved. It was a terrific-looking coat, a deep gray with a black velvet collar.

End of ancient history!

My mother always got her jobs through this nurses' agency on Staten Island known as the Florence Nightingale Registry, but right from the very beginning of the Dipardi job things were different. Instead of just taking our junk and moving right into the employer's house, Helen was told she had to go to Ewing Hospital in Manhattan to help two attendants pick up an old lady in a private ambulance. That meant Helen and I had to lug our two suitcases and three shopping bags out of the Ritz Hotel and onto the Staten Island Ferry. When we finally arrived at the hospital we were late so these two attendants who looked like a medical Mutt and Jeff team were a little cranky. On the positive side, Mutt and Jeff did have a terrific ambulance. It was a neat white Cadillac with DONOHUE'S EMERGENCY VEHICLE painted on all the doors. And below that they had three big blue stars which, I suppose, was to make you feel it was really an honor to ride in it.

"You can't take suitcases," Mutt said almost right off the bat.

"I'll take whatever I want," Helen blasted, and then both ambulance attendants knew they weren't dealing with any ordinary nurse's aide.

The attendants and Helen went up to some ward and I waited downstairs on the emergency ramp with the ambulance. When Helen and the attendants came back I got my first look at Carmelita Dipardi. It makes me sad to meet my mother's next case when I know it is a sick old lady because it makes me think what chance does she really have. However, I must admit when they brought Carmelita down, she didn't look so bad. She seemed somewhat undernourished, but she had this delicate smile on her face that made you feel she was everybody's grandma. Actually, the thought crossed my mind when I saw her next to my mother that the two of them looked a little alike; they both had very cute features—tiny turned-up noses, and short straight hair and bangs. My mother's hair was brown and Carmelita's was like silky snow, and there was something about the two of them that made me think once upon a time they both meant something special to somebody.

Helen moved into the ambulance and sat on a seat next to Carmelita's stretcher contraption. I was already on a front jump seat surrounded by our suitcases and shopping bags. I just hoped the old lady wasn't in pain. I hate pain and death so much I'm the kind of jerk who even wants a bee to live after it's stung me.

"I want a pillow for this lady," my mother ordered.

"You'll get it," Jeff said, throwing one over the seat. Mutt was already behind the wheel and in a second the siren was screaming and the red light on the roof was flashing. I heard rubber peel, and we took off like a bleached Batmobile.

"Slow down!" Helen bellowed. Mutt eased his foot from the accelerator, but I could see by his face in the rearview mirror that he wanted to whirl around and strangle my mother.

8

"Who is that?" Carmelita asked in a very weak voice, staring at me.

"Chris," Helen said gently. "Chris is my son."

Carmelita kept staring at me and I felt she wanted to tell me something. Her eyes looked like they were saying, "I'm sorry you have to see me like this. It must be hard on you." I smiled at her, wanting her to know everything was okay, but then she rolled her head on her pillow and looked out the side window. We raced down the FDR Drive toward the Brooklyn-Battery Tunnel. It was exciting to ride in an ambulance, and I can tell you all the cars moved right out of our way.

Finally we were out of the tunnel and zipping along through Brooklyn. In another few minutes we started up over the Verrazano Bridge. From the middle of the bridge, off on the left, I could see the high rusting tower of the old parachute-jump ride at Coney Island, and on the right was New York Harbor and the skyscrapers looking like long cement fingers grabbing at the sky. Once we had passed the middle of the bridge, the view was like being in an airplane. Stretched out in front of us was Staten Island.

"There's the old town," my mother said cheerfully to Mrs. Dipardi, as she lifted Mrs. Dipardi's head up. Sometimes my mother can be really nice and other times she's really a pip. I can't figure her out.

The old woman looked out the window with tears running down her face. I could just tell she felt deep down this might be her last ride home.

3

WHEN THE AMBULANCE PULLED UP IN FRONT OF 16 HALF
Moon Street, I knew I had arrived at a new low in
Staten Island architecture. The Dipardi residence
looked like a bungalow that had been through a ty-
phoon but didn't quite make it, and the only thing
near it that looked like it was standing halfway
straight was this row of evergreen trees which had
grown so big they were literally wedged between the
bungalow and the sidewalk.

The house was on a corner lot with a driveway that
was pebbles except for two cement strips that ran up
on each side. I knew the neighbors were nosy because
all of them were hanging out of their windows. Some
were even out on the street, including about seven-
teen brats who surrounded the ambulance like it was
a Good Humor ice-cream truck.

"Hurry it up," Helen ordered as the attendants swung the stretcher gizmo out the back door. I felt terrible for Carmelita the way everyone was staring at her as she was rolled through the crowd and up the driveway. Then slowly she reached out a thin hand, and with what little strength she had left, she managed to lift the sheet so that it covered her face.

"Get out of the way!" my mother brayed, shoving some little kids who were in the way of the rolling stretcher.

"Is she going to die?" a little girl shouted shrilly. "Is Mrs. Dipardi going to die?" I wanted to grab the dummy and toss her over a hedge for saying such a thing because you knew Carmelita couldn't help hearing it.

I had gotten out of the ambulance carrying the suitcases and the shopping bags, and a lot of the kids were looking at me like I might be important. When I stand up straight I'm sort of tall for my age, and I have long, straight dark brown hair which I flick from side to side of my face in case there's some sort of complexion imperfection. My hair is just the right length so I can hide almost any part of my face except my nose.

"Watch it!" Helen shot at Mutt and Jeff as they carried Mrs. Dipardi up the stairs of the side entrance which was sort of like a porch with a screen door. "Watch it, or she'll roll off!"

There was a lot more commotion and orders flying through the air, but I did catch a glimpse of this one man when the screen door opened. At first I thought it might be Lloyd Dipardi, but this guy was too old. Suddenly he came charging past everybody out of the house making these strange sounds. He was clutching a black cardigan sweater around him as though he was freezing to death, and he was squealing, "*Eeeh! Eooh! Carmie! Carmie!*" It was so weird, because he had this yellowish wig sitting on top of his head which still had a base circle of his real white hair, and he ran around this cheap-looking vinyl pool to the left of the garage. The garage doors were open and I caught a glimpse of a yellow Ford with black pinstriping on the front fenders. A minute later I caught up with all the confusion in the kitchen, and I didn't know what to look at first. My mother and the two attendants looked mildly petrified, staring at this hairy guy in a T-shirt who had to be Lloyd Dipardi. He looked like he was about thirty years old with enough muscles to beat up everybody within a ten-mile radius. He just stood in the center of the room looking asocial. And sitting at the kitchen table was a boy about my age who looked like a nice kid. He looked more bashful than me and was engrossed in cutting up string beans and putting them into a pot. A big bottle of Wild Turkey bourbon also caught my eye because it was in Lloyd Dipardi's hand.

"I was told you had to work today," my mother said, using her best guilt-inducing tones. Lloyd just looked at Helen as though he might smack her over the head with the bourbon bottle. "I was *supposed* to work," he said in a low, calculating voice, "but I decided to get loaded for the occasion." Then he moved slowly toward the stretcher which the attendants were holding. He reached out and lowered the sheet from the old lady's face. Carmelita Dipardi just looked up at her son with her big red eyes, and I could see tears were still streaming down her face. Lloyd leaned over and kissed her on the forehead. "Hi, Mom," he said. "It's good to have you home."

At that moment the old guy with the twisted face in the black cardigan sweater came running back into the kitchen and he was now sort of doing circles and opening his mouth as though he was going to say something to the old lady, but he didn't.

"Who's this?" my mother asked.

"My father," Lloyd said.

The old man ran off then and disappeared down a hallway, and I got a little worried because I noticed Helen was grinding her teeth. My mother only does that when she is going to do something drastic. I took another look at the muscles on Lloyd and I decided she'd better not do anything too drastic or she'd be unconscious. I jumped when the timer bell went off on the kitchen oven clock as though announcing the start of Round One at a prizefight.

"Shall I get the pot roast out?" the boy inquired, glancing up from his pile of string beans.

"Hey, your mother's not eating pot roast tonight," Helen told Lloyd. "She's on a fat-free diet."

"But you told me to make pot roast. It's your mother's favorite," the boy complained to Lloyd.

"Where's her room?" Helen asked, ignoring the culinary complications.

14

"At the end of the hall," Lloyd said, pointing.

The medical Mutt and Jeff team started to roll Mrs. Dipardi in the direction Lloyd indicated, but Helen let out a shriek: "Wait!" The attendants halted as she charged by. "Unless her room is up to snuff and has clean linen, blankets, and a proper oxygen tank system, she's not staying here." Lloyd burst into laughter, which stopped Helen for a split second, then she continued marching down the hall and out of sight. I heard her flicking on light switches, and everyone in the kitchen just watched Lloyd laughing as he poured himself a fresh shot of Wild Turkey bourbon. In a minute Helen was back.

"It's a good thing you got the air mattress," she said. "Your mother's got bedsores."

"Then get rid of them," Lloyd ordered, his laughter suddenly halted.

"There are some other pains I can't soothe," Helen said. "Only someone she loves can do that," she added, looking straight at Lloyd.

The attendants started off, rolling Carmelita in the direction of the hall. Then Helen's eyes zoomed like sidewinder missiles and landed solidly on the kid who was fiddling with the roast on the stove. He was doing something very theatrical with a ladle and a bottle of Gravy Master.

"Who's this?" Helen demanded.

"That is *Harold*," Lloyd said, going over to the kid and stopping him from adding any more Gravy Master. "Harold, say *hello* to Nurse Boyd."

"Hello," Harold said.

15

"And who's *that?*" Lloyd asked, indicating me like I was from a species other than teenager.

Helen cleared her voice. "The Registry told you my son was coming with me."

"Oh, yeah, I forgot," Lloyd grinned.

"There was supposed to be you and your mother and father. They didn't say anything about a kid," Helen remarked.

I was sure glad Mutt and Jeff came back at just that second because I saw Helen's teeth grinding. Mutt just went out the porch door without even saying good-by.

"She's in the bed," Jeff said.

Helen hesitated, then clomped off and disappeared down the hall.

"We propped her up and made her real comfortable," the attendant said.

Lloyd took a twenty-dollar bill from his wallet. "Here, get a couple of beers," he said.

"Thanks!" the attendant said, grabbing the money and slamming the screen door behind him.

For a moment Lloyd simply looked at me—and I looked at him. He had this tight, curly black hair that made him look like an inebriated gorilla. He finally turned and loped off in the direction Helen had gone. I set the suitcases down, shrugged, and glanced at Harold who was still working at the stove. We smiled at each other and we both pretended we couldn't hear the blaring from the rear bedroom.

Harold and I exchanged a weird nod that reminded me of the kind of expression beaten-down slaves shared in those old movies about flesh traffic from

Africa. I gave him a little wink and motioned him to come along with me in the direction of Helen's still-booming voice.

"Chris and I need at least a half hour every meal so we can eat!" she was saying. "And I'll be cooking for your mother. She's on a special diet."

By now, I knew Harold was on my side. We had slid along the hallway and I was able to peek into the room without being seen. Carmelita was lying in the rented hospital bed and Lloyd was standing by her side. There was also a folded wheelchair against the wall but I didn't think that was going to get much use.

"Hey Ma, can I get you anything? Is there anything you want?" Lloyd asked Carmelita.

"No, son," Carmelita said in a shaky voice.

Helen started some of her nursing chores just to establish her position right from the start that she was the nurse and nurses like to take charge. She checked Carmelita's blood pressure. That was one of her favorite duties—puffing up the armband and watching the mercury fall. Then she opened up the drapes to let some sun in and put some water in a begonia plant and then cranked up the bed. "You just relax and let me take care of everything," Helen told Carmelita.

I could feel Harold right behind me edging closer to get a peek at what was going on in the room, and at just that moment I noticed Carmelita's eyes were open and staring at my mother, but she didn't seem to be looking at her face. Carmelita seemed to be looking at the top of Mother's uniform. I mean, it was weird to see this old lady's head rising like the moon and staring at Helen's chest. Usually, if you crank someone up, they look you right in the eye or they're busy sipping milk or something. When Helen whirled to get a glass of water for the old lady, I noticed her nurse's uniform had come apart at the neckline. A couple of snaps had popped and it seemed like Carmelita just couldn't get her eyes off the snaps. See, that's the kind of thing I always pick up on. I notice it about very young kids and I notice it about very old people. They're always looking at something you don't think they're looking at. Like there could be a three-foot mouse sitting on a chair but instead of noticing that, they'll be looking at a pencil on a table.

Harold tiptoed back up the hall toward the kitchen. I didn't want to leave yet because I was still waiting for some reaction from Lloyd. He took a swig of bourbon from the bottle in his hand.

"I'm going to take care of you, don't you worry," my mother fussed over Carmelita. "You're a wonderful person, I can tell," Helen continued soothingly, wiping perspiration off her patient's brow with a cotton pad. "And it won't be long before you're up on your feet just like the good old days," Helen said, trying to lift her spirits.

At that moment, old Mrs. Dipardi stopped looking at the open snaps on my mother's uniform and turned her head toward Lloyd. The old lady's eyes seemed fragile and sweet as she looked at her son, and it seemed as if she was summoning up energy to speak. At first I thought I was hearing things.

"Did you get a good look at her balloons?" Carmelita asked Lloyd. She kept looking at Lloyd, and then she asked him again, and this time her voice was louder than a whisper. "Did you get a good look at her balloons?"

4

NOW I MIGHT AS WELL CONFESS RIGHT HERE THAT LLOYD Dipardi wasn't as bad as I made him sound. Actually, what he did look like was a filled-out older version of Michelangelo's *David*, slightly off kilter, and fifty pounds heavier from eating too much linguine. And I guess I initially made him sound awful because he really scared me. There was this primeval and mystical presence that he emitted with his total being, and his eyes just stared right through me like he could read my thoughts. What I'm really confessing to you is that I felt a strong and mysterious power in this man and it scared me.

Anyway, after I heard Carmelita ask Lloyd if he had gotten a look at my mother's unmentionables, I was shocked and tiptoed back to the kitchen to rejoin Harold. It had been a long time since I thought of my mother as a female, even just in anatomy. The last time was when I was eleven and the thought first really crossed my mind that my father must have had at least one romantic tussle with her or I wouldn't have been born. I knew there must have been some problems in that department, otherwise my father wouldn't have flown the coop when I was such a tot. The older and wiser say that when there are problems in a marriage you can trace it to some lack of physical expression of love.

"Where's my son's room?" I heard Helen bleat out at that moment from somewhere in the hall.

"Up there," Lloyd answered.

"In the *attic?*" Helen asked in disbelief.

Ugh! I thought to myself.

"I'll be right down," Helen called in to me. Then I heard her and Lloyd stomp up the attic stairs.

"Lloyd's got a great stereo," Harold said to me proudly.

"No kidding?" I said, and before I could stop him, he started giving me a guided tour of the house.

Now, I hope I can do this domicile justice, because it was one of those places you have to see to believe. The kitchen was right next to the porch. It had a toaster-oven which looked like it formerly belonged to Madame Curie, a sink that looked like it did the dishes for a 1944 prisoner-of-war camp, and a dinette set done in precisely the shade of Leatherette impoverished couples select when they've just gotten married and think things are going to get better later on, but they don't. But Harold looked as proud as if he were showing me through the Rembrandt Room at the Louvre. He even opened the refrigerator door and all I could see was a container of milk, two cans of tuna fish, and a few thousand cans of Schaefer beer. A big crystal chandelier hung over the dinette set.

"It's on a dimmer," Harold explained. "Lloyd fixed it himself." He pressed a fat round switch on the wall and then turned the knob to make the chandelier's festoon of lights go from dim to bright and back to dim again.

"That's really something," I said. Then I just blurted out, "Who *are* you?"

"Oh, I'm Lloyd's best friend," Harold said matter-of-factly while leading me into the living-room area, which was hardly separated from the kitchen area. I mean, there were no walls. "Lloyd's got two speakers out here for parties, but the turntable's in the bedroom with the records and four other speakers."

"Great," I said. I could tell by now that it was a strain for Harold to think and talk at the same time because he walked into a coffee table. Then there was a whole wall of books which were dusty. In fact, the most valuable thing in the living room was this thing they call a "tallboy," which is like a plain old cupboard you keep in a living room, but nobody uses the word "cupboard" anymore.

"What's in there?" I asked.

"Lloyd's booze supply."

Harold slid a key out from under the tallboy and stuck it in the lock. He swung the cabinet doors and let me tell you, there was all the best Gordon's gin, Wolfschmidt vodka, and Wild Turkey bourbon that

23

any kid could want, including a shelf for after-dinner drinks like saki which is what you use to tie one on if you are of Oriental persuasion.

"Lloyd must have a lot of loot," I said, exploring.

"He makes good money at the shipyard and there's no mortgage on the house," Harold explained. "Shipyard workers make more than a lot of professors, you know."

Harold returned the key to its inspired hiding place beneath the cabinet, and then took me over to this mushroom pool table. Needless to say, it was the main feature of the living room. You usually only see them in the most low-life kind of bars where it costs about a quarter a game to play.

Harold delicately opened the door to a room at the far end of the living room and led me inside. It was Lloyd's bedroom.

"That's a McIntosh MQ 101 environmental equalizer, a Sony mixer, and a United audio turntable," Harold said, pointing to the area to the side of the bed. I admired the stereo equipment, but then I focused on the bed. It was queen-sized, covered with a spread featuring an artistic weaving of a phosphorescent, snarling jaguar.

Then I spotted this corner of the bedroom which had barbells, a scale, and a padded bench. Some of it looked like ordinary torture equipment, but behind it were the records, so I started flipping through them.

"Lloyd likes hits of the past," Harold said. "He's read all those books in the bookcases too."

"That is, before he started reading liquor labels," I said smugly.

24

Harold acted like he hadn't heard that remark but I got a funny suspicion that Harold was a lot smarter than he looked. I might as well confess something right now. The truth of the matter is I would have given my right earlobe to be as good-looking as he was because he had flowing straight blond hair and a big open smile.

"Lloyd's buying me a new tooth," he said.

"That's nice," I said.

"It's a molar but I'm still self-conscious about it," Harold said.

"I'm self-conscious about my nose," I offered.

"There's nothing wrong with your nose," Harold said.

"I think it's too big. It's a little like my father's nose was." That was another faint memory I had of my father. I remembered his nose was larger than mine and I wanted mine to grow up and be just as big. I have the feeling, though, his nose was actually just normal for a man's face.

At that moment I happened to notice that the bathroom had two entrances, one from Lloyd's room, and the other led out into the hallway just at the bottom of the attic steps. I could see that was to be my door.

"I had nits, too," Harold explained.

"Oh?"

"That was before I met Lloyd."

"What was he, a nitpicker?" I quipped.

Harold laughed. "I also had malnutrition," he added, leading me back to the living room. Suddenly we both snapped to attention. Lloyd and Helen were clomping down the stairs and we both looked to see if either of them had any black eyes. They didn't. They both just ignored us and marched back down the hall to Carmelita's room.

"I trust the attic meets with your approval," we heard Lloyd say to Helen.

"I love the unfinished look of it," Helen crackled, and by then they were out of earshot. Harold continued then.

"I was a physical mess when I met Lloyd but he taught me how to take care of myself and eat the right foods," he clarified.

"You must spend a lot of time here," I said.

"My mother and father live two blocks away over on Elm Street but I like it here. Sort of hang out. Listen to music, cook for Lloyd, clean up a little. Do the wash," Harold said, placing bamboo place mats on the table.

"You mean you like being the resident *slave?*" I hadn't really meant to say that. It sort of slipped out. "I'm sorry," I apologized.

"That's okay," Harold sputtered. He started to fold napkins nervously.

"How old are you?" I asked him.

"Sixteen."

"Sixteen!" I underlined vocally. "*Sixteen!* I'm fifteen and I'd never try cleaning up this dump."

"This isn't a dump," Harold said defensively.

He finished the table and began to wash some plates that were piled up in this old, cracked porcelain sink. And then in a voice of strength and conviction, he said, "You don't understand; I want to do it. It was Lloyd who took an interest whether I ate right or not. I wouldn't be standing here now if he hadn't taught me the ropes. Wait. You'll see. They don't make people like Lloyd anymore."

I suddenly looked at Harold in a new way. I realized that Lloyd had a powerful hold on him. It took me twelve seconds to get it out, but I finally said, "Look, Harold, I'm sorry I said anything." And I really meant it. He looked like he was mulling it over. Then I added, "Let's just be friends, okay?" Slowly a smile came across Harold's face and we shook hands and laughed.

"I have to go to the store," Harold said. "If Lloyd wants to know where I went, tell him we're out of heavy cream, okay?"

"Okay," I said. Harold flashed me another smile and ran out of the house. I saw his head disappear past the kitchen window and I figured anybody who trusts you enough to tell you he once had nits can't be *all* bad.

5

AS SOON AS HAROLD WAS GONE, I RAIDED THE REFRIG-
erator. I found two pieces of spiced ham and a jar of
pigs' knuckles hiding among the beer cans, and I was
just taking a sip of milk right out of the carton when I
realized someone was watching me. I almost choked.

"In this house we use a glass," Lloyd said.

He came right over and took the carton out of my
hand. He wiped the rim of it and put the container
back in the refrigerator. After a moment he calmly
took a stogie out of a box on top of the refrigerator.
He lit it, staggered into the living room, and stretched
out on the sofa. "Where's your old man?" he asked,
his eyes looking like liquor mortis was setting in.

"He's dead," I said.

He continued to stare at me. "I'm sorry to hear that.
Did your mother knock him off?" he asked with a
grin.

I let Lloyd have his laugh. I just sat down at the kitchen table and felt him watching me.

"You must feel badly that your mother's sick like that," I asked him.

"Your mother's sick, too, but in a different way," Lloyd sounded back. I grabbed a Ritz cracker out of the box on the counter. Lloyd continued questioning me. "How old were you when your father died?"

"Almost six," I answered, "but he left us a few months before that."

"You mean when he couldn't take your mother anymore," Lloyd said.

I got up and shoved a whole Ritz cracker in my mouth and munched defiantly. "If you'll excuse me, I think I'll retire to my suite."

"Hasn't anyone told you not to talk and eat at the same time?" he asked.

"No. No, they haven't," I said, stopping short and looking at him.

"See, your father would have told you that," he said.

"How do you know what my father would have told me?" I asked him.

"I can just look at you and see," Lloyd said, as if he was omniscient.

"And what else can you see?" I asked.

Lloyd looked at me a moment. "I see a boy unprepared for life."

I hadn't the faintest idea of what he was talking about, but just the way he was observing me made me feel very, very uncomfortable. I felt like I was being judged but I wasn't sure what my crimes were.

I started for the stairs and said, "Well, I'll be seeing you."

"Don't forget your junk," Lloyd added, pointing to the corner in the kitchen where I had dumped the suitcases and shopping bags. I picked up the stuff and I must confess, at that moment I had the feeling that it was very, very important that he like me, but Lloyd wasn't letting up. "Do you have a girl friend?" he quizzed in a peculiar tone.

"Of course I have a girl friend," I answered.

"What's her name?"

"Vivian Smith," I invented.

A smile curled itself on Lloyd's face. I really felt like telling him to shut up and act like all the other people whose houses we invaded. When Helen and I went into a house, nobody grilled me about my girl friends. They asked things like what do you like in school, or what baseball team do you root for? You don't meet a kid and right away ask about his amorous activities. Strangers aren't supposed to get nosy right away with a kid but that's what made Lloyd different.

When I got to the middle of the living room I turned around and said, "I've got *three* girl friends."

Lloyd took a big puff on his cigar and gave me a demonic wink. "Good for you," he said.

At that moment my mother appeared at the top of the stairs. "Upstairs! Upstairs!" she commanded. "Give Lloyd privacy in his own home," she said.

At the top of the stairs I saw there were two parts to the attic. The right side was an unfinished area and

31

had a lot of trunks and junk piled in it. But the left side was a real room with a slanting roof that would have been great for anyone who had a posture of forty-five degrees. The only place I could really stand up straight was in the middle of the room. And the bed was arranged so that if I had a bad dream I'd bolt up and bang my head on a rafter. But it was really clean. Harold had obviously gone crazy with a sponge mop and there was a hint of Raid fragrance lurking about. I had to admit, the sheets were nice and fresh, and when my mother checked them for bugs, she couldn't find a single one.

"You'll be very comfortable up here," Helen said. "I'm sleeping downstairs on a cot in the old lady's room."

"Will you be okay?" I asked.

"I'll be fine," she remarked. "But there's something about the setup here that doesn't sit right with me, so don't get too comfortable."

I noticed there was one prefabricated cardboard closet in the room that was pretty good for hanging up clothes if you were a midget. Helen took over one corner for her suitcase and shopping bags and I just tossed my suitcase on the bed. It really didn't make much difference whether I packed or unpacked because the only things really good in my suitcase were a pair of sneakers that looked like they were recycled and my father's chesterfield coat which, like I said, I always took with me no matter where we went. I always unpacked my father's coat because I figured it'd last longer that way. I also liked to brush the velvet collar and try it on at least once a week to see if it fitted me better.

"I have to go to the bathroom," I said.

"There's only one bathroom," Helen said matter-of-factly as she rummaged through her suitcase. "We can't just go whenever we feel like it."

I watched Helen fuss over her things, and I felt this old sickening feeling start in my stomach, the one I got sometimes when my mother started a new job. "Well, if you'll excuse," I said, heading for the top of the stairs.

"What do you have to do?" she asked.

The sickening feeling grew. "I said *I have to go to the bathroom.*"

"Just a leak?"

I nodded affirmatively and weakly.

As loud and domineering as Helen could be, when it was just her and I in a room in a strange house, she sort of became a nervous little girl. It was at those moments when she seemed most vulnerable that I felt closest to her. We shared a common bond. Then, after a few minutes, to compensate for her weakness, she would become so paranoid, you'd think the police were going to come and drag us off to concentration camps if we used somebody's bathroom at the wrong time. That was her problem. Half of her was like Attila the Hun and the other half was like a kid afraid of the dark.

"Here's the milk bottle," she said, taking the familiar object from a white plastic bag and handing it to me. I accepted it helplessly and she kept unpacking as though she knew what I would say. Helen always brought the milk bottle with her. It was always the same one in a plastic garbage bag. And unless we were on a case where we had our own private bathroom, she'd always make me use it.

"I don't want to use this anymore," I told her. "I'm getting too old, Mom."

I had been complaining for over a year about her bathroom routines, but this time I tried to be stronger about it. I knew for some reason, in this house especially, if she made me use a milk bottle it would fill me with so much shame I'd want to die. Helen could be eccentric and crazy in other ways, but this thing I never could understand. Maybe it's all right to make a kid do things like that when they don't know any better, but by now I was certainly old enough to know that milk bottles were intended to contain milk. Nevertheless, I really had to take a leak so I just turned away and used it.

Suddenly music began to play downstairs. I could tell from the vibrations that it was coming from Lloyd's bedroom. I didn't recognize the song, but some corny male vocalist was singing something about a love affair that had gone wrong—and there were a lot of violins playing trills in the background.

"He's down there," Helen said quietly, almost frightened. "Can you hear him?" She sat on the edge of my bed and began to peel off her white stockings.

"Yes, Mom," I said, "I hear him."

6

THAT FIRST EVENING LLOYD AND HAROLD WEREN'T HOME so I watched TV in the living room while my mother made some sandwiches for us out of the pot roast. After that, Helen gave the house the once-over, running in and out of Carmelita's room to make sure the poor lady ate all her supper, drank her tea, and had some cookies. Helen always wore one-hundred-percent Dacron white uniforms on the job in case her patient did something like throw cream of asparagus soup on her. "Wash and wear" was her motto right down the line.

Every time something exciting came on the television set, like when there was going to be a hatchet murder or some policeman being falsely blamed for shooting a minority member, Helen would barge in and warn me about Lloyd. She said I shouldn't talk to him, that I should never be alone with him, and that I should keep away from him, because there was some-thing sinister about him. She also said I should stay away from Harold because she thought he was a poor waif who had fallen under Lloyd's evil spell. She said she also thought he was a teenage nurd. Mom was very emotional about this subject.

By nightfall, I looked in on old Carmelita and she really looked terrible or maybe she was just bored, so I thought I'd better try to strike up a conversation.

"What do you think of Frisbees?" I asked. Carmelita's eyes moved slowly downward so that it looked like she was staring at her sheet. I didn't ask it to be sarcastic, it's just that I had really been thinking a lot about Frisbees lately. She didn't answer so I went to adjust her oxygen tubes. I'm not trained for any great medical emergencies, but Helen taught me how to do the simple stuff like regulate oxygen flow and make sure an intravenous needle is stuck in right—and to take a pulse. The one thing I can really do is tell if someone's dead.

I know I was mistaken, but there was a second while I was near Carmelita when I thought she tried to punch me. It was just that her little left hand came up, shook in the air, and then tried to land on my jaw.

"What's going on in there?" Helen bellowed from the front of the house when she heard me let out a short scream.

"Nothing," I yelled down the hall.

I could hear Helen rummaging about in Lloyd's closet and bureau drawers. She was undoubtedly go-ing through his bedroom like a ferret. After that, I heard her running up and down the attic stairs. I knew she was up to her old tricks.

"Don't tease her," Helen yelled in counterpoint to her foraging noises.

"She tried to sock me!" I called out.

"That's all right. But keep it down," came her appreciation of my humor.

That was the kind of conversation Helen and I usually had anyway. Even when I'd tell her the truth she wouldn't recognize it. Then the door next to the old lady's room opened and Lloyd's father came in yelling, "Carmie, Carmie, I had a bad dream," and then he ran right back out, loping down the hall like a kid who lost his way home. It's sad to see old people act like babies again. I followed him until I got his attention.

"Hi, Pops," I said. He grunted and went back in his room.

It didn't take me long to learn Pops did everything on the hour, the half hour, and the quarter hour. He'd light the oven, he'd stick in a TV dinner, he'd boil water, he'd go to the bathroom. One time while he was out in the kitchen staring at a tea bag, I peeked into his room and saw he had three alarm clocks lined up on his bed stand. He'd set them, and you'd hear an alarm go off, and then, *bang!* the door would open, and it'd be just like some kind of Swiss barometer where a witch pops out when it's going to rain.

The big treat of the evening was that Helen allowed me to use the bathroom. "He's not home. Get in there and do what you have to do," she said. Then I went up to the attic and tried to get to sleep. I was just about to close my eyes when I heard Helen tiptoe up the stairs. She stood in the doorway looking like a white goblin.

"Are you sleeping?" she asked.

"No," I said.

"I just wanted to say good night, Chris."

"Good night, Mom," I said.

She sat at the edge of my bed and put her hands through my hair a minute like she would do when I was a little boy. "I just want you to know that I think this nice old lady might not make it."

"I understand, Mom," I said. Then she got up and went downstairs.

I turned over, and I must have been sleeping all of forty minutes when a whole lot of nocturnal sounds woke me up. It started when Lloyd and Harold came home. Lloyd must have been high because he started singing "Ain't Misbehavin' " in three-quarter time. Then someone put on a big-band version of "You Make Me Feel So Young" on the stereo, and in a minute I could hear Lloyd singing right along. After that, I heard my mother and Lloyd screaming at each other for a minute or two in the hall. At the stroke of midnight, Pops popped out of his room going "Carmie, Carmie, Carmie!" Finally everything seemed pretty normal, and this time I thought I was really going to get to sleep, but I heard some rustling noises. I looked out the attic window and there was a black Volkswagen parked behind Lloyd's Ford. Some sailor and a girl were rolling around on the lawn giggling, doing sensuous gyrations, and drinking beer. Around three A.M., some kids roared by the house screaming at the top of their lungs: "Hey, Dipardi! Hey, Dipardi!" A little after that another car went by the house three times in a row and this time there were some other kids yelling curses that I can't write in this confession. One of the kids threw a beer bottle that shattered on the cement steps between the pine trees at the front of the house. Just after that, there were so many little noises going on in the house I took my pillow and lay in the dark at the top of the stairs, like I used to do when I wanted to hear my mother talk to a neighbor about her problems. The floor was so hard I figured I'd need an orthopedist if I fell asleep in that position, but I didn't want to miss any of the action. And to tell you the truth, my ears were being strained to capacity.

As it turned out, all I heard was Lloyd telling Harold about his adventures or misadventures during his travels to Buffalo, New York, and there were lots of shadows sort of moving around the hall. The only thing beyond that I really understood clearly was that some precious silver dollars that had belonged to his grandmother's collection were missing. "Somebody stole them!" Lloyd kept slurring. "Somebody stole them!" he said over and over again between gurgles.

The whole next day I didn't see Lloyd because he was working the day shift at the shipyard. And Harold told me he wouldn't be around either because he was going to spend the day with his mother and father. He was also interested in buying some bay leaves from the A&P because Lloyd had told him bay leaves were used in the old days by this ancient Greek lady who would chew them, inhale fumes from a volcano crack, and then utter profound prophesies.

"How would he know a thing like that?" I asked.

"*Those*," Harold said, pointing again to the dusty books lining the living-room walls. "Lloyd used to read all the time at the shipyard because all he has to do there is keep an eye on an air compressor. All he says now is that books are baloney. All except cookbooks, that is!"

"Don't your folks think it's moderately abnormal that you almost live over here?" I finally asked.

"Oh, no," Harold said. "They like me to get out of myself. Besides, they're glad I don't have nits or malnutrition anymore." Harold smiled proudly. "They even like Lloyd. My mother's a bartender at the Sea Skift Inn and my father works as a shoeshine man on one of the Staten Island ferryboats. He likes to grow tomatoes."

Suddenly the oven timer went off again.

"The cauliflower's done," Harold said, leaping up and taking a pot off the stove. "I make a very good stuffed turkey."

"Great," I said.

"I can also make goulash and stuffed peppers. My mother taught me how to do those. She's Czechoslovakian with bleached hair." He was now running around the kitchen with cooking tongs and it was all I could do to keep my mouth shut.

"I find it very relaxing," Harold clarified, as the cauliflower plopped into a ceramic dish. "Lloyd's mother is a good cook. See, Carmelita used to have this other house in Rosebank, but when they knew she was sick they sold that house and that's why there's a few of her things in the house, like the chandelier and things like that. She refused to come unless he agreed to put up her chandelier. It reminded her of home." Harold sprinkled something that looked like Vitalis on top of the cauliflower. "It's going to be a cold vinaigrette," he explained.

"Why are you cooking so much food?" I asked.

"Lloyd's got some friends coming over tonight."

"Some people from work?"

"No. Just some kids." Harold turned the light off on the stove. "So why don't you and I go to a movie or something? I don't feel like being here."

"Why? What's wrong with them?"

"Oh it's nothing," Harold said. "I just don't feel like serving all those kids tonight."

I could tell Harold wasn't telling me the whole truth. Then, in the next minute, Harold had jammed the turkey into the oven, shoved some leftover pot roast in a large Baggie, and dashed out the door to see his folks.

Around two P.M. Helen told me she was going out for a little stroll and that Carmelita was sleeping soundly. I was glad to be practically alone because it would give me a chance to snoop around Lloyd's medicine cabinet. Medicine cabinets reveal the most intimate secrets about people, like if they have the heartbreak of psoriasis or use antifungal aerosols. The worst thing would be if old Mr. Dipardi wanted to use the bathroom, but I would hear him coming a mile away.

Lloyd's bathroom cabinet was pretty mundane. He

had a regular razor, the kind that uses double-edged blades. And he used a mentholated shaving cream, and a roll-on deodorant. I didn't find the stuff in his bedroom particularly revealing either. All his underwear was stacked neatly. Everything seemed in its place. The bedspread was nice and neat with the phosphorescent jaguar staring at me. Then I found myself flicking my hair this way and that because I was sort of nervous just being in his bedroom. So I got out. Around two-thirty Helen came back carrying some daisies which she put in a vase and set up in Carmelita's room.

I watched the usual afternoon lineup on television: a couple of movies and a game show which had a lot of underprivileged contestants jumping up and down because they were winning things like a set of enameled chopsticks or a Yamaha motor scooter. Then Harold came back around six and said we were catching an eight-fifteen flick. I must admit I was a little bit curious about who was coming over, but I decided I'd rather go to the movies than be uncomfortable with people I didn't know.

Around seven-thirty I was up in my room putting on a pair of jeans, and I found a T-shirt I had forgotten about that said KICK ME on the back of it. That's when I heard yelling from downstairs. It was Lloyd's voice booming in his bedroom which I realized was directly below. I didn't want to be nosy, but I thought I might as well lie down with my ear against the floorboards. Lloyd was telling Harold he had no right going out because guests were coming over, but Har-

42

old explained that was the only way he could get me out of the house and that he'd already set up the buffet with napkins, silverware, and radishes peeled to look like flowers. Lloyd still insisted Harold had to stay home and serve the turkey.

"I'll carve it before I go," I heard Harold groan.

"Then it'll dry out. And where's the cranberry sauce?"

"We don't have any," Harold said.

"We had *two* cans!" Lloyd bellowed. "Two cans!"

I could tell by the stomping that Lloyd was heading into the kitchen with Harold trailing him. They were still yelling at each other all the way, and I had to hand it to Harold—he was really giving it back. While I was lying on the floor I noticed a few feet from my head a couple of floorboards were loose. They were just under the bed, and the boards didn't seem to be nailed down or anything, so I wiggled over and found they just lifted right up. I could really hear the voices good now, particularly when they stomped back from the kitchen after a fruitless cranberry-sauce search. And I really didn't mean to be prying but there was some fiberglass insulation just under the boards, and I always wanted to see the way fiberglass was put into floors so I lifted it out. I was surprised to see a crack of light coming up from below. I leaned forward and put my eye to the crack. I was very embarrassed because I realized I was now looking down on the top of two heads. I felt like a bat in their belfry.

"Then let Chris come to the party," Harold was saying.

"No. He wouldn't fit in." Lloyd went into the bathroom. "Have you seen any soap? I just bought four bars of Dial!"

"In the medicine cabinet," Harold said.

"They're not here," Lloyd complained. "They're gone like my silver dollars."

I heard Lloyd slam something, and Harold disappeared out of my view. Then I heard another loud crash, and this time there was a growl and the slamming of some more cabinet doors.

"Where's my Head & Shoulders?" Lloyd was bellowing.

"Maybe it's in the bedroom," Harold said.

I couldn't see what was going on down there, but it sounded like Lloyd was ripping everything apart. It sounded worse than Helen when she's rummaging through a house. And I may be dumb, but it doesn't take me that long to put two and two together. Lloyd's voice got louder and my heart almost jumped out of my throat when I heard the thumping of feet on the attic stairs. I yanked my head out of the floorboards so fast I almost knocked myself unconscious on one of the bottom slats of the bed. I threw the insulation back into the hole and slammed the upper floorboards back into position. I managed to look something like a hunched-backed troll when the attic door flew open and Lloyd charged in. Harold was hot on his heels looking ready to help prevent boy-slaughter. Lloyd halted, his nostrils twitching. The words he said came like the gentle tremblings before an all-out earthquake.

"Where's my stuff?" he asked.

"What stuff?"

"You know," he said, clenching his fists and taking a step toward me.

Harold cued me in quickly. "There's a bottle of aspirins, some shampoo and cranberry sauce, and a few other things that are missing."

"Where are my silver dollars?" Lloyd specified, closing in on me.

"I didn't take anything, Mr. Dipardi," I said. I sat on the edge of the bed keeping my eyes cast down on the floor and I caught sight of the milk bottle in the corner of the room.

"He didn't take anything," Harold said.

Lloyd bounded suddenly to the side, grabbing my mother's suitcase. He practically tore the zipper open, and there was a spray of Helen's clothes in the air. It was sort of like a bomb going off at a JC Penny remainder sale. Lloyd clawed through the stuff, enraged that there was no contraband. He grabbed my suitcase.

"Let go of that!" I yelled. And this time I was mad! I tried to shove him, but he gave me a *thwack*, and I went flying back onto the bed. After throwing my valuable wardrobe into the air, he spotted my father's coat and ripped it off the hanger to search through the pockets. I went at him again.

"Get your hands off that! Get your greasy hands off it!" I screamed. He had the overcoat searched in less than two seconds and threw it over my head, tossing me back down. I tried to sock him, but he grabbed my arm. This time I landed on the floor, and it hurt. He bounded around the room and then found something I didn't even know about. It was a special plastic shopping bag wedged on one side of the portable cardboard closet. The bag ripped under the strain of Lloyd's yank, and cans of cranberry sauce, jars of mushrooms, a couple of packages of Lipton soup, handkerchiefs, silver dollars, bars of soap, a bottle of shampoo, books, aspirins, and a canned ham went rolling across the floor. Lloyd turned his eyes on me and a terrified Harold ran around scooping up the haul.

"I ought to smack you right in the face, you little thief," Lloyd said, coming at me again.

"Leave him alone," Harold pleaded, shuffling around on his knees.

Lloyd turned to Harold. "Get out of here!"

"It's not his fault. Leave him alone. Don't punch him."

"I'm not going to punch him."

"Yes, you are."

"I said I'm not! Just get out of here!"

Harold looked more frightened than I was as he finished gathering up the loot. I mean, it was all pretty stupid, now that I think of it. Harold standing in the doorway with a bottle of Head & Shoulders and a canned ham peeking over his forearm; Lloyd, barefoot, with his drunken shipyard-worker's face looking ready to annihilate me. And me, on the floor, holding on to my father's coat like it was the Golden Fleece. We all froze.

"I just want to talk to him," Lloyd said. Harold waited a moment longer, and then started out of the room. He looked at me again to see if I was all right, and then he said softly, "It's little stuff. It's just little stuff." Harold was still mumbling, going down the stairs, "It's little stuff," but at least he had gumption and was good enough to stand up for me, even though he didn't know I wasn't guilty.

Lloyd noticed a silver dollar Harold had missed; he bent over, picked it up, and put it in his pocket.

"Are you enjoying your little visit?" Lloyd asked, his eyes shooting arrows into my face.

"It's like a resort," I said.

Lloyd looked around the room again; his stare came to rest on my scattered possessions.

"I don't like boys who steal," Lloyd said.

"I didn't steal anything from you."

Lloyd kept his eyes glued on me as I rose slowly from the floor, put my father's coat on a hanger, and hung it up on a rafter. I smoothed out a few wrinkles and checked to make sure Lloyd hadn't ripped any of the pockets when he rammed his big fat hands in them. Then I just went and sat back down on the bed with my head against the pillow and my arms behind my head. I wasn't going to let any sauced-up shipyard worker know he had scared me in the least. Finally, Lloyd spoke out loud and deliberate. "I know you didn't take it, kid. I can see you've got some sense of character, but that mother of yours. What kind of example can she set?"

"My mother doesn't need anything of yours," I said, sticking up for her.

"Dial and silver dollars just don't collect in plastic bags. Your mother's got an illness. Can't you see it now?" Lloyd said.

I jumped up off the bed. I thought how dare this drunk judge my mother, even though I knew Helen had sticky fingers. We stared at each other. I felt a territorial right in my room, even though it was his house. Then Lloyd came toward me, but this time I didn't flinch. He stretched his arm out and patted me on my shoulder. "You're all right kid. Your heart's in the right place but you don't know if you're coming or going." He started out toward the door, but before leaving, he turned around and said to me, "Where'd you dig up that coat? It's too classy for you. And too big. You should have gotten one that you can fill out. That one's for a man." Then he was out of the door.

I screamed after him, "It was my father's coat, you jerk," and I slammed the door so hard that I hoped the sound would shatter his eardrums. I stood still and listened, thinking he would charge right in on Helen and accuse her, but I think he must have felt too ashamed of the mistake he had made accusing me. I really hate it when anybody accuses me of doing something I didn't do. I hadn't stolen anything since I was six years old, and that was a twenty-five-cent Woolworth's Mother's Day pin. I was still fretting and clicking my tongue in anger when I heard the doorbell ring. There were some strange voices, and I thought I heard the laughter of a young girl. I just lay on the bed like a petrified mummy and the only thing that made me feel good was seeing my father's coat swinging near the window. Every time I stand up for my rights I feel bigger, and every time I let people walk over me I feel smaller. I just lay there, wiggling my feet for another ten minutes, until I

heard Harold's voice from the bottom of the stairs.
"Hey, Chris?"
   "What?" I yelled.
   "You ready to go out?" Harold asked.
   "You bet I am," I called back down.

7

HAROLD AND I DECIDED NOT TO GO TO THE MOVIES. WE
ended up going to South Beach, riding the bumper
cars and having pepperoni pizzas. Most of the time,
though, I was trying to think about what Lloyd's problem was in the joy-juice department. There seemed to
be no point in asking Harold, because by now every
time I quizzed him he went cross-eyed and did things
like drip hot mozzarella under examination. And he
was being such a good guy I didn't want to really
pressure him. What I did ask him about was that
crew that arrived just before we went out. There was
this one kid, by the name of Bob, who looked like a
teenage wrestler. Of course, that was only my first impression when I was introduced to him real quick by
Harold. And Bob had a skinny teenage girl with him
named Quily. Her family was Greek and I had never
met a Greek girl before, especially one named Quily.

The scene was, as Harold later explained, that this Bob, the wrestler, always went to the Maypole Bar in St. George, which is right near the Staten Island Coast Guard base, and sometimes he'd pick up a girl or some friends and they'd all come out to Lloyd's for a home-cooked meal and free drinks. Then along with Bob and Quily was this girl by the name of Rosemary who was a junior in high school. All I said to her was hi. She was going through Lloyd's record collection when I came down, and she just said hi back. She seemed very sincere. She also seemed sophisticated, with eyeliner and loop earrings, and she even complimented Harold on his turkey. As for Lloyd, he still looked angry when we left, but Harold didn't seem to mind. He said Lloyd often had a lot of strange people in the house and he couldn't take them all the time.

After the pizza, Harold insisted on a beer at the Surf and Turf Inn. I didn't think we'd get served, but as it turned out the Surf and Turf Inn serves anyone not attached to an umbilical cord. This place was the pits in entertainment so I convinced Harold to go back to Lloyd's.

The minute we got off the bus at the corner of Half Moon Street we heard the stereo blasting from the house. It sounded like a really wild party was going on. As we walked up the driveway, I noticed red underwater lights playing on Lloyd's plastic back-yard pool, making it look like it was just waiting for some human bodies to flail around in it with reckless abandon. Before we went in I checked out the window of Carmelita's room. It was half open and I saw my mother was lying on her cot having a cigarette and reading a copy of *National Lampoon*. She had really made the room cheerful with flowers and stuff, but I knew she was fuming over the racket coming from the front of the house. Then Harold and I went in and there was still only the same crew as when we had left.

It was Lloyd's turn at the pool table.

"Five ball in the side pocket," Lloyd gargled, giving Harold and me an all-is-forgiven wave. Then he chalked the cue stick so hard the chalk broke in half and he missed the shot anyway. Quily, the Greek girl, let out a laugh, but it was phony and conniving. In fact, she had such a nasty laugh Lloyd took his cue stick and gave the sofa a smack with it.

"Lloyd's been losing," Rosemary whispered to Harold and me.

She was just sitting at the kitchen table looking even more sophisticated than before and smoking a Winston.

"How much?" Harold wanted to know.

"About fifty dollars," Rosemary said.

Harold fixed me a plate of food and a King Alphonse, which in other parlance is half heavy cream and half Kahlúa liqueur. I could see Rosemary was very impressed which was just what I wanted. "I drink them all the time," I told her. We were still munching when Bob finished off the pool game and started braying euphorically. Then Lloyd put his Greek record on the phonograph and Bob and Quily started dancing these Greek dances.

"Look, I think we'd better stop," Rosemary said. "It's getting late."

"It's not late," Lloyd said, beginning to dance around the room.

"Lloyd, your mother's sick," Rosemary pleaded.

"Not to worry," Lloyd said, and started singing along with Bob and Quily. The rest of us just sat around the kitchen table eating smartly and sipping drinks. They were now doing one of those really authentic Greek dances where everybody lines up in a chorus line doing these dips and stamping their feet and doing squat kicks. In a minute Bob was twirling and balancing a glass on his forehead. Quily was allowed to turn the music up even louder and I was surprised at Lloyd's inconsiderateness for his sick mother. Then Lloyd dashed over to the chandelier dimmer switch, turned the lights down, and suggested that everybody go out in the back yard and dip in his suburban vinyl pool.

I could tell Rosemary was disturbed about the whole thing because she just excused herself and went into the bathroom.

Bob had apparently had enough whammo water to click right into the mood. He started taking off his clothes and then ran out the back door with Quily, yelling "Yippee!" And in another minute, all you could hear was splashing and yelling out in the back yard—which I knew was going to go over really big with Helen. With them out of the house, Harold turned down the stereo and we just sat eating. I could hardly see my plate the way the chandelier lights had been turned down so much, so I leaned over and turned the dimmer switch up.

"Turn that light down!" Lloyd brayed from the pool like a walrus.

I jumped at the sound of his voice but Harold beat me to the switch. He turned the lights down so that now the chandelier looked like some kind of ghostly upside-down Christmas tree.

"What's his problem?" I asked.

Harold groaned, "The bright light goes right out and hits the pool."

"So what?"

"Lloyd doesn't like people to see he's a little fat in the belly. He only likes the dim red lights."

"Hey, Harold! Bring out some sangría!" came the barking voice again from outside.

Harold looked at me and shrugged. I could tell half of him didn't want to do it, but the other half loved the idea of being able to grab a bottle of Almadén Red Mountain claret, add some frozen grape juice and lemon wedges, and pull out the long-stemmed wine glasses.

"Don't do everything he says," I told Harold.

"I don't mind," Harold said, but it sounded more like an excuse just to go out and keep his eye on Lloyd.

I leaned over and deliberately turned the chandelier switch a full revolution. A blast of light ignited the kitchen and spilled out into the back yard.

"I'm going to knock somebody's block off!" Lloyd screamed from the pool.

Harold quickly turned the dimmer back down and gave me a pleading look.

Paul Zindel

"Sorry," I yelled back to Lloyd in a comical voice and the words were already out of my mouth before I realized if Helen heard me she'd come running out of the back room and lock me up in the attic like a bat.

"Hurry up," Lloyd's voice clanged out. A second later Harold was scooting out the door with a tray of glasses. He was no sooner gone than Rosemary came out of the john and headed for the bottle of Almadén Red Mountain claret.

"Want some?" she asked, pouring herself a bit.

"A couple of fingers," I said, wanting to demonstrate that I had some savvy about the inbibing of alcoholic beverages, but I could tell she didn't know what I was talking about. She brought me over a glass and sat next to me on one of the Leatherette specials. She had obviously freshened up her makeup because now she looked like a contestant in a Miss Teenage America contest, and she smelled delicious. I hoped maybe she did it for me.

From where we were sitting, we could look right out the kitchen windows and barely make out the figures in the pool. It looked like a pack of frolicking schizo kids. And Harold was serving wine to everybody right in the pool.

"Lloyd must really not like his mother," I said.

"You're wrong," Rosemary corrected me. "He went up to that hospital twice a day for three months. You don't do that if you hate somebody. It got so we were afraid he was going to commit suicide. Bob and I went with him a couple of times when he was too exhausted to drive."

56

"Or too drunk," I said. And I no sooner had the words out of my mouth than I knew I'd said the wrong thing.

"You'd drink too if you found out your mother was dying. And he's paid all the bills and given her everything she needed. He worked double shifts for a while until he collapsed."

"I'm sorry. I didn't know," I said. But the one thing I did know was that I was beginning to like Rosemary. She seemed to be the kind of girl who always sticks up for the underdog. I suppose what I liked about her most, aside from her looks, was her directness. She looked right in my eyes when we talked, and when I spoke, she really listened like I had something important to say. That made me feel really good because I've talked to girls who would drift off in their minds and daydream about buying a skirt or sweater for a Saturday night with someone else. But not Rosemary. She seemed to live moment to moment.

"Are you Bob's girl friend?" I asked, just to break the ice.

"No," she said. "We're just friends now. He was the one who introduced me to Lloyd."

"Oh really," I said. "Are you and Lloyd good friends?" I asked with a lump in my throat.

Rosemary was chasing a speck of cork she'd spotted in her drink.

"Lloyd has lots of friends," she said, then quickly changed the subject. "Your mother must be a very brave person," Rosemary said. "She has a lot of guts to take care of sick people. I sometimes visit old Mr.

Dipardi in his room. Bring him cookies or something. It's disturbing, and his stroke isn't half as bad as some of your mother's expatients'."

"How do you know?" I asked.

"I was talking to her," she said.

"You spoke to her?" I gulped.

Rosemary took another sip of her wine. "I brought Mrs. Dipardi in some tea before and your mother and I struck up a nice chat. She seemed very friendly, but she asks so many questions."

"Like what?" I asked.

Rosemary took another sip of her wine.

"She kept asking me this and asking me that, so finally I told her I was pregnant."

"Are you?" I asked.

"No," Rosemary said, lighting a cigarette. "But I knew it was the kind of thing she'd like to hear."

We both burst into laughter, and we must have laughed for five minutes straight. Then Rosemary asked me seriously: "Are you anybody's boyfriend?"

"No," I said. "I used to go out with a girl by the name of Nordine Ditmer, but she got fat."

"Were you in love with her?"

"Deeply."

"Well, you don't stop loving someone because they get fat," she said.

"She hit two hundred pounds," I lied.

"Your love sounds a little superficial to me," Rosemary remarked. "How long did you go with her?"

"Almost a year. The whole time I went to Port Richmond High School."

"You went to Port Richmond High School?" Rosemary asked enthusiastically.

"Yes," I said. "I also went to Curtis, New Dorp—and next September I'll go to Tottenville. I'm the only kid I know that went to that many high schools."

"I go to McKee Vocational," Rosemary said. "I was going to become a cosmetologist. Did you ever ask your girl friend why she got fat?" She leaned forward in her chair as though she was really obsessed with this tale of obesity. Then I felt she was checking my complexion so I flicked my hair so it covered most of my face.

"That wasn't the main problem," I said slowly. "The worst thing was that she was half Polish and was ashamed of it so she went around making believe she was half French."

"What's wrong with being half Polish?" Rosemary asked.

"I didn't say there was anything wrong with it," I defended myself. "I just said that *she* thought there was something wrong with it."

"Did you *really* love each other?" Rosemary wanted to know.

I put my wine glass down on the table and decided to be honest about the whole thing. It makes me nervous to lie for extended periods of time.

"No. She didn't love me," I finally confessed. Rosemary looked at me like she was going to ask why I lied at first, but she didn't.

"Then why'd she go out with you?" she asked with sincerity.

"Because nobody else would ask her."

"Why not?"

"She was so beautiful everybody else was afraid she'd say no."

I noticed Rosemary lean back a bit and she seemed really interested. "Then what made you think she'd go out with you?" she asked me.

"We sat next to each other in English class and we had some good laughs."

"So then you didn't go out with her just because she was pretty. She must have had a good personality," Rosemary pursued.

"I guess not. You see, I was desperately in love with her but she was only using me."

"Using you for what?" she probed.

"To take her somewhere or help write her term papers. Bring her Pepto-Bismol from the drugstore. Things like that. She was the only girl I ever loved. After we broke up, I stayed in my room for weeks."

Rosemary seemed profoundly moved by my flop in the romance department. "I was used once, too," she said bitterly.

"You too!"

"Yes. His name was Billy Quinn."

"Billy Quinn?" I asked.

"Yeah. Do you know him?"

"No."

"Oh. Well, he was treasurer of the junior class at McKee High," Rosemary explained, "and after dating me for two months he asked my best friend for a date to this big party they were having at Ray Diamond's house on Lighthouse Hill. I felt terrible. First I was hurt for myself. And mad at my girl friend for accepting the date. Let me tell you, Billy Quinn was the cat's meow, if you know what I mean. He had the looks, he had every athletic letter in the school, and his father was a doctor. And the only thing I couldn't figure out was why out of the blue, he invites my best friend to this high-class bash. But I found out."

"What do you mean?"

"Well, it turned out to be a Pig Party, that's what I found out"—and her voice was very, very sad—"where boys have a contest to see who can date the ugliest girl."

"You're kidding."

"I may be kidding, but let me tell you, my girl friend—Gertrude Bang—won first prize at that party, and there wasn't any kidding when they presented her with a real, live baby pig right in front of everybody. All the boys thought it was such a hoot until Gertrude had plastic surgery on her nose and they did her chin too while they were at it. She turned out so beautiful, all those guys including Billy Quinn kept asking her out, but she only laughed in their faces. So you see, I know about the world of appearances and how cruel people can be."

The noise out at the pool got so loud we couldn't ignore it anymore. It was a terrible racket, and I wasn't the least bit surprised when Helen charged into the living room. First she gnashed her teeth at me.

"When did you get in?" she asked, turning the chandelier lights up to their full brightness.

"Just now," I said.

61

"Well, go up to bed," she ordered.

"Shut that off!" Lloyd roared from the pool.

"Who does he think he is?" Helen erupted. She barged right out onto the back porch and threw open the screen door.

"He's drunk," Rosemary warned.

"Mr. Dipardi!" my mother screamed out in the direction of the pool. "If you don't stop this, I'm going to call the police!" Her voice dribbled into surprise so I knew she'd gotten her first gander that they were all nude. "You're disgusting!" she said, marching back into the kitchen and giving the screen door another slam. It was the first time I had seen my mother's face turn red in a long time.

"I mean it!" she yelled in a sort of multidirectional way, which I suppose was intended to disguise the fact that she had been caught off guard. "I will call the cops," she reiterated, "and we'll see what they think of this."

Lloyd burst into the house with a green towel wrapped around him.

To overcome her nervousness, Helen said, "Your mother is sick in there. She has taken two sleeping pills and a Demerol and still can't fall asleep with all this racket." Helen took a deep breath and tried to switch into a lower gear.

Lloyd grabbed a fresh bottle of Wild Turkey.

"Lloyd, I think you've had enough," Rosemary said, going to him and gently taking the bottle away. Helen zipped around like a muskie going for a worm. "Even if you don't care about your own mother, there are laws against exposing kids to the kinds of things you

62

do around here," she said. Then she darted back out into the kitchen and switched on the chandelier until the whole cluster of bulbs and crystal drops flooded the room. It was like somebody had set off a giant flare. Lloyd charged straight at Helen, knocked her to the side, and shut the light off.

"What do your neighbors say?" Helen interrogated.

"It's none of your business what the neighbors say! You work for me, so get back in there and work!" Lloyd ordered.

"I don't work for you, I work for your mother!" Helen replied in a very stern voice. Her eyes grew bigger. I think she knew she was out of her league.

"Mr. Dipardi," Helen continued, "your mother needs some peace. The party's over." She walked out on the porch and yelled to the kids, "Do you hear that? The party's over!"

"Hold it," Lloyd corrected her. "The party's just starting." Then he let out another laugh. "Did you get that, Nurse Boyd? *Dipardi's* just started. Got it? And if I didn't need someone to take care of my mother, you'd have been thrown out the moment you walked in, son and all. But my mother seems to like you."

"With these working conditions it would be hard to find anyone willing to put up with all this, so who's doing who the favor?" Helen asked.

"Mrs. Boyd," Lloyd said with a strange smile on his face, "I'm paying you a good salary, so why don't you go earn it and mind your own business."

"I see what goes on here, Mr. Dipardi, and I'm telling you, you are a very sick man. My responsibility is to take care of your mother but I see things."

Paul Zindel

"And what do you see?" Lloyd asked her.

"I'll tell you what everyone else on this block already knows," Helen said with utter disdain. "I went for a walk this afternoon and I've met some of your neighbors. They know from my white uniform what I'm doing around here, and they all want to know how Mrs. Dipardi is doing. There are cards and gifts in her room from many of them. And what I want you to know, Mr. Dipardi, is that your neighbors all tell me what a wonderful woman your mother is—and they told me what they think of you, Mr. Dipardi!"

"I know what they think of me and I don't care," Lloyd said, taking another swig of liquor.

"Your neighbors see young people coming in and out of this house, but they don't want to become involved in anything unpleasant. But I don't feel that way. Unless you start keeping a clean ship here, for your poor mother's sake, and bring some respect back into this house while she is still under this roof, I'm going to blow the whistle on you. I'll press charges, Mr. Dipardi. Yes, I'll press charges that you're corrupting the morals of minors!"

Helen stared at Lloyd. She breathed in so deeply it looked like she doubled in size, and her hand reached out. She turned the chandelier-switch on so bright it now seemed like a hydrogen bomb had been detonated. Even Harold froze at the sink, staring at my mother's hand, glued to the light switch. And then in what seemed like less than a second, Lloyd was on his feet, a kitchen chair was in his hands, and the chair went up into the air, arching through the room. There came this terrible crashing sound and sparks began to fly. Bulbs exploded! The whole house shook. And there was Lloyd, hurling the chair, crashing it against the chandelier, socking it time and time again as pieces of crystal and glass and sparks rained all over the room. We all threw up our hands to stop the hot flying glass from hitting our eyes. Five, six, seven times, Lloyd hurled the chair against the chandelier until it was out for good.

The party was really over now. Bob looked so depressed as he came in and saw what had happened. He was sort of high and just picked up his and Quily's clothes. Quily obviously had the good sense to stay and get dressed outside. Finally, Lloyd just let go of the chair and flopped down on the sofa.

"Go to bed," Helen ordered me.

I was ready to protest when Rosemary spoke up loud and clear. "I think we'd all better go home." It was wonderful the way she just took charge of getting everyone out. I walked about an inch at a time toward the attic stairs and Rosemary and I exchanged a lot of sophisticated looks even while she was heading for the screen door and telling Harold to fix Lloyd some coffee.

"Good night, Mrs. Boyd," she even thought to say. "I hope I see you again soon." I might have been projecting but again I hoped it was something she was really saying for me.

Helen backed me into the hall like a lion tamer rescuing someone from a cage. She shooed me up the stairs and then made a beeline for Carmelita's room. About fifteen minutes later I had finally gotten undressed and into bed, but my heart wasn't really into sleeping; it was more like into doing push-ups in my chest. And I waited for my mother to come up and tell me we were going to clear out. When she didn't, I knew who was going to be boss at Half Moon Street. At least for the time being.

I lay in my bed so bedazzled thinking about everything that had happened that night—from Quily making sneaky little smiles to Rosemary blinking her fantabulous eyes to Lloyd's smashing of the chandelier—that I didn't remember about the crack in the attic floor for almost an hour. When I did remember, I got right down on my knees, lifted up the floorboards, and carefully took out the insulation. I stuck my eye down to the slit to see if anything was going on down in Lloyd's bedroom, but nobody was there. I got back into bed and I waited another fifteen minutes, and then I heard noises below so I just put my old eyeball back at the crack again. Lloyd had just put on a record, and some lady warbler was singing "Wheel of Fortune." Then I saw Lloyd plop into bed like he was bombed out of his mind. He was staring straight up at the ceiling and I was afraid he could see me, but he couldn't. Then there were sounds like Harold cleaning up the broken glass out in the kitchen. Lloyd yelled out something about how he thought somebody robbed a bottle of his booze. Then he complained he had cut his foot on a piece of glass. A lot of small talk without much philosophic depth. At least four records played, one worse than the other. I tried to listen real carefully, but it was hard with the music playing, and with Lloyd being so drunk. When I finally caught a drift of conversation, Lloyd was complaining about a knock in the engine of his car. He said his car was a rotten lemon and that he had been stuck and he was having trouble with the insurance company, and if the insurance company didn't behave themselves, he was going to go down there and beat everybody up. Harold walked into the bedroom and turned the records over. I thought I heard my name mentioned and I tried to get my ear as close to the crack as possible.

"What do you think of Chris?" Harold had asked Lloyd.

"What do you care what I think of him? He's your buddy," Lloyd said, grabbing some Wild Turkey and pouring it into a water glass.

"I was just wondering," Harold said, "because you seem to have made quite an impression on him."

Lloyd looked like he was contemplating the universe for a moment, then I heard what he said. I heard it very clearly.

"He's a nurd," Lloyd said. Then he asked Harold to turn off the kitchen lights on his way out.

"I'll clean the rest of the stuff up in the morning," Harold said as he closed the door to Lloyd's bedroom. I heard the screen door squeak as he left the house.

After that I couldn't hear or see anything else so I just stuck the insulation back and laid down the floorboards again. I didn't care whether he heard it or not. I mean, sometimes some things happen in your life and you just don't care about anything—and that's how I felt. I got back into bed and I felt very cold. I let myself freeze for about five minutes as though I wanted to punish myself for being such a loser, and then I finally got up, took my father's coat off the hanger, and pulled it over me as a blanket. It felt so heavy and warm. And I had a dream. A wonderful dream about Rosemary—that we would fall in love and live happily ever after.

8

ANYWAY, THE MORNING AFTER THE CHANDELIER HAD GOT-
ten socked like a Mexican piñata, I came downstairs
and watched Harold sweeping up what was left of the
shattered crystals. Harold was wearing gym shorts,
sneakers, and a pair of bloodshot eyes. Lloyd was still
sleeping it off and Harold told me Lloyd had decided not to go to work at the shipyard. Harold also
let me know Helen had had a grueling night with
Carmelita so they were all still sleeping too. I didn't
want to tell Harold that I knew my mother'd been up
almost the whole night because when I came down to
try to use the bathroom around three o'clock in the
morning, she caught me and yelled at me for making
noise, and chased me back upstairs and told me to use
the milk bottle. That ticked me off so much I didn't
get to sleep until after four myself. Like I said, the
only reason I had been able to get to sleep at all was

thinking about Rosemary. The more I thought of her
the more terrific I thought she was. Of course I
couldn't think of Rosemary without remembering Nordine Ditmer. Really beautiful girls usually don't seem
to be able to feel sorry for anybody, but that was one
kind of feeling I knew Rosemary understood. Actually, Rosemary reminded me of another girl who used
to sit next to me in general science. This girl was always nice to me. She always smiled and sometimes
she'd give me half of her ham sandwich. One day she
even invited me over to her house after school and
she played the "Moonlight Sonata" for me on the cello.
And then after that, her mother made her play a Hungarian Rhapsody. She was the only girl in the school
who could play the Hungarian Rhapsody on a cello.
Her name was Peggy Darbeziac, and she and I were
terrific friends until she and her family moved away
to Frenchman's Legg, North Dakota. And the funny
part about it is, the day after she moved I realized I
could have fallen in love with her. When she was
around, all I could think of was Nordine. But when
she was gone, I realized how I wasted my time thinking about the past when I could have shared something terrific with Peggy. In fact, she and her cello
were more lovely inside than Nordine ever was, and
she was even nicer to me. What a dope I was. Have
you ever done that? Built someone up in your mind
so much that you make a hero or heroine out of
them, then no one else can ever be as good? I decided
I had been a real stupo.

When I came out of the bathroom Harold was still
cleaning the kitchen in his gymnastic costume so I

poured myself a bowl of Sugar Smacks and milk. I had a lot of things to ask him by now, but I had to make sure I didn't ask him about anything I'd only have known by snooping. I also really felt that Harold wanted to be my friend and I didn't want to hurt him. If he knew that I didn't like Lloyd it would all reflect on him and he'd feel worse than I was sure he already did.

"Does Lloyd always have kids over?" I asked. "I mean, like Bob and Quily."

"Not really," Harold said.

"Quily looked like a real weasel," I commented. "She looked like a friend I had at New Dorp who would steal dogs from blind people."

"I thought you didn't have any friends," Harold caught me with.

"Oh, I had a few friends until I found out they were criminally crazed," I clarified. "They'd really work Lloyd over," I added.

Harold looked at me with suspicion and then went back to sweeping. "Lloyd knows how to take care of himself."

"They'd just party with him and get him drunk. Then they'd walk out with everything that wasn't nailed down."

"Lloyd's gotten ripped off a few times," Harold admitted. "And he got beat up twice. Once by a cop and once by a marine."

"No kidding," I remarked, then I continued with, "Why are all these strange people attracted to Lloyd? Look, Harold, you're sixteen and Lloyd is around thirty." I was really going to lay it on the line but then

71

a whole bunch of interruptions started. Helen had to call the doctor to tell him Carmelita didn't want to take any more of the pills that were keeping her heart going. I could tell from the way Helen was talking to him that the doctor told her to force Carmelita to take her pills. I know, from all her jobs, that my mother didn't believe in mercy killing. Then while all this was going on, old Mr. Dipardi burst out of his room in his black cardigan sweater calling out, "Carmie! Carmie! You've come home too late to make dinner again!" And then he went into the kitchen area and stuck four of Mrs. Paul's frozen fish sticks into the toaster-oven, spilled some Special K, and then popped back into his room. He hadn't once appeared at the party. Then Helen was running in and out emptying the bedpan. Two minutes later the phone rang. Harold was busy cleaning the mess old Mr. Dipardi made so he asked me to grab the phone before the ringing woke Lloyd up. It turned out to be Rosemary and I was sure glad to hear her voice. She was just checking to make sure everybody was okay, and she seemed particularly concerned about Lloyd. I told her he was still sleeping, and she thought that was good.

"You know, Christopher, it was great meeting you last night," she said, sounding even more worldly than ever.

"The pleasure was mine," I insisted.

"Then let's be friends—okay?" Rosemary said, and she sounded extremely sincere.

"You bet."

"Maybe I'll see you tonight," she said.

"Great," I said. "I mean, that would really be great."

When I hung up from her, old man Dipardi reappeared just to get his fish sticks and I poured myself another bowl of Sugar Smacks and this time drowned them in chocolate milk. Then a thought hit me. "Doesn't Lloyd have an extension phone in his room?" I asked Harold.

"I unplugged it so he could sleep," he said.

Finally, I finished my cereal and decided to converse further with Harold. "Do you have any money?" I asked him.

Harold looked up in surprise. "What for?"

"I wondered if you could afford to run away."

"Why should I run away?"

"Maybe to California and buy into a Carvel ice-cream franchise," I advised.

"But I like it here," Harold said. He had moved on to preparing a D-Zerta mold in the shape of what seemed to be half of a mongoose.

"You won't like it after Helen gets finished."

Suddenly I noticed Harold freeze. He was stiffer than his D-Zerta mongoose and he seemed to be looking past me. There was a sound and I turned to see Lloyd standing in the doorway of his bedroom looking like Mighty Joe Young. I was afraid Lloyd had heard everything but I tried covering up.

"Good morning," I said cheerfully.

Lloyd gave me a mean look that lasted about a solid half minute. Then he staggered and disappeared down the hallway toward Carmelita's room. About sixty seconds after that we heard Helen screaming. That went on for about five minutes. Then Lloyd came back to the living room rather bright-eyed and bushy-tailed, laughing his head off. I decided I wasn't going to let him interfere with my life in the least so I just sat in one of the decrepit stuffed chairs and started reading a copy of *Mad* magazine. Harold rushed a cup of coffee to Lloyd, who plopped down on the sofa. I just sat there turning every page nonchalantly even though I couldn't concentrate on the jokes with him sitting right across from me. Lloyd finally stopped his gaiety and reached out his hand. I thought he was going to throw his coffee cup at me. Instead, he just set it down on a table and dialed a number on the phone.

"All I know is there's a knock in the engine," he was blasting somebody.

I could see Lloyd's eyes getting to look like a shark's at whatever the guy on the other end was saying.

"You didn't tell me about a deductible," Lloyd bellowed, yanking open a drawer next to the sofa and throwing some papers on the floor. He held on to something that looked like a contract and flipped through its pages. At the same time Lloyd stretched the phone cord long enough so he could pour some Wild Turkey into his coffee while keeping the receiver to his ear.

"Look, Rocco," he finally said, "I've been doing business with you for seven years and if you think I'm going to pay for a valve job on a brand-new car, you're crazy!" Then he shut up and was listening for a while, and I saw the left side of his face twitch. Then he just slammed the receiver down.

"Here," Harold said, bringing Lloyd a dish of the fruit salad.

"How do you like that?" Lloyd grunted. "He sells me a policy that doesn't pay a dime unless I wreck the whole car."

"Maybe he didn't mean to," Harold said.

"He's a crook," Lloyd mumbled, taking a spoonful of the fruit salad. "Whoever heard of a five hundred-buck deductible?"

Harold started doing a few quicksteps and straightened his gym shorts. "Should we exercise now?" he asked, like a freshman looking for a gold star.

Lloyd pulled himself up off the couch. "Yeah, let's get it over with." He started jogging toward the bedroom with Harold trotting after him. "*You* too," Lloyd said, turning back at me.

"I already did my exercises," I mumbled, still keeping my eyes glued on the *Mad* magazine.

"You couldn't have," Lloyd said. Harold stopped in the doorway to see what was going to happen. "You don't have any dumbbells," Lloyd added.

"I'm into isometrics," I said simply.

"Did you ever do arm curls?" Lloyd asked.

"Oh, yeah, I used to do a lot of those," I lied.

"You don't even know what they are," he said, coming right over and grabbing my wrist. "Come on, we'll get your blood moving," he added.

"I've added an inch on my chest," Harold said proudly from the doorway. "Try it."

Well, before I could stop it, we were all in the bedroom and this special little gym class had started up. It was only Harold and me, and our great phys.-ed. teacher did nothing but stretch out on the bed balancing his fruit salad on his stomach. I realized now why

Harold was wearing gym shorts all morning. He dashed over like a roadrunner to the mat and weights in the corner.

"You got gym clothes?" Lloyd asked.

"Sure, but I'm staying in these," I said, adjusting my jeans.

"Tomorrow you work out right," Lloyd said, "and that means shorts, sweat shirt, and sneakers. You wear a jock, too," he ordered. "Come on now, twenty-five deep knee bends to get the system moving." I could sense a jot of extra cruelness in his voice which made me suspect he must have overheard at least part of the unkind things I was saying to Harold earlier.

"I changed my mind," I said. "I think my isometrics were enough." I started to leave the room even though a part of me really wanted to try doing some of the exercises. I never did work out anywhere because nobody ever really taught me how and I really felt like a weakling watching Harold go up and down like he was a pogo stick.

"Well, I think you're a liar," Lloyd said before I could get out of the room. "I think you're a liar like my insurance agent."

"Chris isn't a liar," Harold said between puffs. "He's okay. No kidding, Lloyd."

"Well, you two just go right ahead and enjoy your deep knee bends," I said, starting for the door again.

"Where are you going?" Lloyd asked. "To California and buy into a Carvel ice-cream franchise?"

Harold looked at me and we both then knew Lloyd had definitely heard us talking about him.

"Chris was just kidding."

"That's not called kidding," Lloyd said. "It's called fiction." Lloyd broadcast a great big smile in my direction.

"I'm not a liar," I said quickly.

"Then let's see your muscles."

"I don't see *you* doing any exercise," I said.

"I already did mine," Lloyd stated, mimicking me.

"And I did mine just like you did yours," I told him. And this time he let me get all the way to the door before he really let me have it.

"So long, nurd," he said.

I stopped and looked at him. I had to fight to stop my voice from being shaky. "What did you call me?"

"I think any friends you ever had still have pacifiers in their mouth," he declared.

"Lloyd," Harold said, "he didn't mean anything."

"What are you shaking for?" Lloyd asked me with an even broader grin. Lloyd's teeth were flashing like a barracuda about to swim in for the kill.

"Leave him alone," Harold said, starting to do some sit-ups on the mat.

"Nobody butts into my business in my house," Lloyd exploded. "And where do you come off advising Harold to run away, you little punk," Lloyd added.

I took a couple of deep breaths. "Doesn't it ever seem a little weird that the only people who seem to be able to stand you are kids?" I managed to say.

"Oh, go jump rope, nurd," Lloyd said. Then he turned his attention to Harold. "Come on, fifty vertical leg raises."

"I can't do fifty," Harold said.

"This morning you're doing fifty. Just make believe this *jerk* isn't even here."

"I suppose if I were you I'd be a drunk too," I said.

Harold shot me a warning look, but I didn't care. I told Lloyd, "Without your Wild Turkey and your free shelter for kids to get away from their parents I don't think any kid in his right mind would come see you."

Lloyd let out a chuckle, as though he was above my hurting him.

"You're like a teenage PX. What's on tap for tonight?" I quizzed. "Are you going to beat up a couple of lamps?"

I could see Lloyd's eyes change and get really mean again.

"Maybe I don't have any friends," I went on. "Well, you don't have any either, except Harold—and I don't know how he can stand you." I was surprised at the sound of the strength in my own voice.

"That's it. Perk up a little," Lloyd said. "Be daring and be a man instead of the little worm you are. Let your father be proud of you even if he's dead. That was a very good beginning. Now, beat it, you little misfit," Lloyd said with great control in his voice.

By now I was trembling. "Anything you say, you Pie-eyed Piper," I said.

"Oh, go take a leak in your milk bottle," Loyd said in a monotone.

He flashed a smile as though he had laid down a royal flush. I felt he had shot me through the heart with a bullet. I couldn't stay in the room, but my legs couldn't carry me out. I had really been holding my own until he mentioned the milk bottle—but his knowing about it was so mortifying I had to stop my attack on him and start defending myself.

"My mother makes me do it. She doesn't like me in the way."

"In the *way?*" Lloyd picked up on, joyously. "Why, Chris old boy, you're not in the way around here. You fit in as snug as a bug in a rug. Right, Harold?" He kept his eyes riveted on me. "I like teenage misfits, as you already pointed out. You *are* a misfit, you know," he said with a sudden frightening coldness.

I looked at Harold, and if ever I needed a friend, I needed one then.

Lloyd just continued. "You see, Chris, Harold was a freak when he first came here. Weren't you, Harold?" he asked, sitting up on the edge of the bed and taking another mouthful of his fruit salad. "Harold was a hundred-and-ten-pound weakling when he came but now he can beat up any kid in this town."

"Well that's terrific. What if he doesn't want to beat up any kid?" I asked. And this time I almost made it out of the room. Lloyd sprang like an animal, grabbed me by my shoulders, and slammed me up against the door.

"I'm not finished with you," Lloyd said, "you see, because there's a few things I've been wanting to tell you, and one of them is that you're retarded. Do you understand that word?"

"Please don't," Harold practically begged. "Just let him go, please."

I felt like I was in a nightmare. I thought I was hearing things, that the words flying through the air had nothing to do with me. I felt my shoulders going numb from the pressure of his hands. Before I knew what was happening, Harold was right behind Lloyd and he looked ready to give him a karate chop if he had to.

"What do you mean, I'm retarded? You don't even know me," I inquired, my vocal cords so tight I thought they would snap. I flicked my hair trying to hide my face.

"I mean you're out of it," Lloyd said. "Is that clear enough? You don't know anything about anything. You don't know how to hang up your clothes after you take them off. Or about polishing your shoes. Have you ever looked in the mirror when you walk? You droop over. You don't even know how to take pride in your body. You don't know the first thing about being a man. And I'll tell you, your father would drop dead again if he saw you pissing in a milk bottle. All I know about your father is that he picked out that nice coat and he was smart enough to leave that witch of a wife. Unfortunately, you didn't have that much luck. That's why you need a lot of help now. Help your father would have given you."

I nodded that I understood, but I really didn't.

"You see in this world, there are kids who are taught how to take care of themselves and survive, and there are those kids who missed the boat."

"My mother is far from perfect but at least she always was there for me when I needed her," I blurted out.

"And if you keep going, you'll wind up like her, an adult misfit," Lloyd said.

I felt like I'd been punched in the stomach.

"I mean *look at you*," Lloyd said. "You make a terrible appearance. That T-shirt looks like rigor mortis set in, and anyone can see that you've never flossed your teeth in your life. You take no pride in yourself. You don't like yourself. I hope this doesn't offend you because it's just a little fatherly advice," he added with a weird smile.

"Well you're not my father" was all I could say.

"That's right, kid, but if you had a father, you might not be such a loser. It breaks my heart to watch you," Lloyd said.

"Consider yourself lucky then that *your* father was around," I managed to say.

"There's being around and being around, kid, if you get what I mean," Lloyd said. "Let's put it this way, I was not father's favorite son and I was his only child. So maybe we have more in common than you think."

I almost passed out but I thought I saw the barest trace of humane understanding in his eyes.

"Do you have anything else to say to me?" I asked, thinking I must have been mistaken. "Any more of your constructive compliments?" I asked defensively.

"Yeah," Lloyd said, "trim the hair around your ears."

Harold was getting uncomfortable. "Lloyd, come on, we've got to get the car fixed," he said to change the subject. "It's late."

Lloyd reached into a pocket of his pants and gave Harold his set of keys. "Here. Start the car. I'll be right out."

"Don't say anything more," Harold said, pleading. "Leave him alone. *Please?*"

"Get out of here," Lloyd ordered. Harold ran out the back porch slamming the screen door. With Harold gone there was nothing to prevent the tears from rolling down my face. I stayed smack against the door like I had been crucified. Lloyd looked at me long and hard.

Suddenly Helen's voice rang out from the back room. "Mr. Dipardi, I need some relief." At the sound of her voice I faded back into the bedroom. I just wanted to croak. *Please everyone just go away and let me disappear,* I said to myself.

Lloyd watched me start crying and I really felt like a nurd. Then he spoke, and for the first time he sounded as though he didn't loathe me.

"The next time she tells you to use a milk bottle, you tell her what to do with it."

Lloyd reached forward and gently brushed the hair out of my face and it seemed as if we were looking at each other for the first time. It really took me off guard, as though I had just finished a big fight with my father about using the family car or something and my father was sorry about being so rough on me. I always hear that from kids who have fathers. Sometimes fathers go berserk over their sons getting their hair cut or putting out the garbage or something like that and then after they're all finished yelling they give their sons a hug and a few dollars and tell them they're sorry. I mean, I was absolutely amazed at the change in Lloyd. Like he had suddenly seen something in me that he liked. Something worth saving, I hoped. And at the same time he looked terribly sad, but the funny part was I didn't get the feeling that he was sad for me so much as he was feeling sad for himself. I mean, it was really baffling, to tell the truth. Then he just turned and walked out of the house. Suddenly I heard Helen yelling all the way out to the garage from the window in Carmelita's room.

"I'm supposed to get a few hours off, you know! When are you coming back?" She sounded absolutely bonkers.

Lloyd bellowed his reply from the driveway. "As soon as I drive a long Ford off a short pier!"

9

SOMEHOW I MANAGED TO PUT THE PIECES OF MY GUTS TO-
gether again and make it back upstairs to the attic. I
lay on my bed for hours. I didn't care if I ever moved
again. I didn't think I even deserved to walk the earth
anymore and certainly not during daylight hours. I
felt like some sort of nocturnal horror. At one point
Helen called upstairs, but I didn't answer. I kept my
eyes glued to my father's coat which still hung from
the rafter near the window. It swayed phantomlike in
a breeze which somehow managed to wiggle through
the room. I kept trying to remember every word
Lloyd had said, to consider it and think of what I
should have said, but I kept wanting to forget. I
wanted to cut off my power of memory and think of
only the best things I could. I imagined I was on a
tropical beach with palm trees swaying and natives
coming up to sell me coconuts with a shot of rum in

them. But Lloyd's annihilating voice kept intruding. I felt as though I had only gotten a few jabs and he had managed to pound me with a pneumatic drill. Something he had said would rush to my mind, and then I'd think of a retort, something to really hit him where he lived. But no matter how I reenacted the scene, I couldn't win. And always, what I remembered most was the end when he reached out and brushed my hair back. Now was the first time in a long time that I really, *really* missed my father.

Finally around six-thirty I heard old man Dipardi hobbling down the hall going "Carmie, honey! Where's the chutney?" and popping his TV dinner in the toaster-oven. Then I heard Helen running around a bit. At one point I heard her in Lloyd's room, so I figured she was looking for a few more things to steal. My curiosity got the better of me then, so I looked down through the crack in the ceiling and saw Helen had stripped the sheets off Lloyd's bed and was putting a rubber mat on the mattress. I didn't know what she was up to, because then she started making the bed with fresh linen. That held my attention for all of about three seconds, so I got back on the bed and all I could think of was running away. On my own savings I could get about as far as Atlantic City if I was lucky. I thought about filling up my suitcase with Lloyd's liquor bottles and selling them along the way. I could stand on the New Jersey Turnpike hitchhiking with a sign saying SPECIAL DISCOUNT ON WILD TURKEY FIREWATER! A lot of other crazy ideas flashed through my mind, but I decided they weren't

so good either. And finally I was filled with this urge
to just start screaming. I just wanted to lie on the bed
and let out a scream at the top of my lungs until the
men with the white coats came to put me in a strait-
jacket and take me away. After entertaining that
thought for about a minute and a half I decided I
already was in a nuthouse. The thing I really needed
was to escape from myself, because I think I disliked
me more than I disliked anybody. I needed time; just
a little time to figure out how a kid escapes from his
own head.

By eight o'clock I felt I had enough strength to get
up off the bed. I could hear my mother still mess-
ing around downstairs. But I didn't care. I took my
toothbrush out of my suitcase and the milk bottle from
the corner, and I went down. As I came into the hall I
was almost run over by Helen who was rolling Carmelita along in a wheelchair, right into Lloyd's bedroom.

"Where have you been?" Helen wanted to know.

"Sleeping," I said.

"Good. Now you can watch the poor gal awhile during my break. She hasn't shut up a minute."

My mother didn't notice the milk bottle in my hand.
But I didn't care whether she did or didn't. I went
right out the back porch and threw it so hard into a
garbage can it broke. When I came back in, I just
barged right into Lloyd's bathroom and started brush-
ing my teeth. By this time Helen had rolled the
wheelchair into a position right next to Lloyd's bed.
She saw me through the open door.

"Help me lift her," she demanded.

I rinsed my mouth, and then went into the bedroom. "Where?" I asked.

"Into the bed, where else?"

"In *Lloyd's* bed?"

"It was her bed when he took it over, and she's been groaning about it all day. She wants to be in her own bed."

Poor Carmelita was looking up, listening to every word and nodding macabrely, but I don't think she understood anything going on.

"Did you ask Lloyd?" I inquired.

"I don't ask that maniac anything." Helen went back down the hall and I decided I was going to take a shower, so I went back in the bathroom and shut both the doors. The water wasn't splashing over me for more than two minutes before I heard Helen open one of the bathroom doors. "What do you think you're doing?"

"I'm getting washed," I said.

"I don't want you in there," Helen reprimanded. "He ought to be back soon."

"I'm still getting washed," I said.

"Get out of there."

"Look," I said. "I'm going to use this bathroom whenever I feel like it," I called out over the noise of the spraying water. There was no response so I didn't know whether Helen heard me or not, but a minute later I heard the oxygen tanks on their trolley clanking along into Lloyd's bedroom.

"Don't get snotty with me or you'll be sorry," Helen finally said when she heard me turn off the water.

"The old lady's on six liters of oxygen per minute now, and when that drunk gets home you tell him there's no smoking in this room. Let *him* sleep in the rear room."

"You tell him," I said.

"I'm not going to be here," Helen said. "I'm going out for Moo Goo Gai Pan."

"What?" I asked, getting out of the shower with a towel around me.

Helen threw open the door between the bathroom and Lloyd's room. "I haven't had a break all day, and I'm going down and eat a good Chinese dinner. You just take care of Carmelita. I don't care if the house decays while I'm gone." Helen went back to the bed and began rolling Carmelita like a human bean bag as she tightened the bottom sheet.

"What if she needs an injection?" I asked, picking up my dirty clothes.

"Then turn her over and give it to her in the tush!" Helen took her pocketbook and began to fix herself up a little in the mirror on Lloyd's bureau. I ran out the hall door and upstairs to the attic. I dug some clean clothes out of my suitcase and put them on. I had a pair of slacks that looked like $2.99 Korvettes specials but they were clean and there was a fresh blue pullover terry-cloth shirt. Then I remembered Lloyd's medicine cabinet had a couple of men's deodorants, after-shave lotions, scissors, and shoe polish, so I went back downstairs and started sprucing myself up. I decided I would never give anybody, ever, the chance to call me sloppy again.

"What are you doing?" Helen asked.

"I don't want to be left alone with her." I decided to be truthful, sliding Lloyd's bottle of roll-on Ban up and down my underarms.

"Well you're going to be. I'll bring you back an egg roll. You know how you love egg rolls," she reminded me.

"I don't want any."

"Here's the doctor's phone number in case she takes a turn for the worse."

"Where?" I asked, peeking out from the bathroom.

"I'll leave it here." She lifted the telephone on Lloyd's bed stand and slammed it down on a piece of paper. "You won't need it," she said, grabbing her pocketbook and flying toward the living room. "I gave her enough morphine to put her on Mars for two hours."

"Was she in a lot of pain?" I asked.

"She's okay," Helen said, but I sensed she was protecting me a little.

By now I'd gotten very used to feet stomping out onto the back porch and the screen door slamming. It seemed like rats running off a sinking ship but I was happy to be alone. I spent another fifteen minutes in the bathroom doing some things like clipping my nails and putting a dose of Dr. Scholl's foot powder into my shoes. Finally, it seemed so quiet in the bedroom I decided I'd better check. I walked around the front of the bed and was expecting to see Carmelita just dreaming away but instead she was propped up looking straight at me. She still really didn't look too bad from the neck up, even though her upper torso looked skinnier than ever. If you just looked at her face and forgot about the oxygen tubes hooked up to her nose, she still looked like an amiable grandmother in bed with pneumonia. Nevertheless, looking at her made me ashamed I'd spent so much time worrying about my problems. I mean, she had big problems.

"Can I get you anything, Mrs. Dipardi?" I said, looking into her wide-open eyes. I wondered what was really going on in her mind. I wondered if I were her what must it be like? Would my entire life be flashing in front of my eyes? I have this theory that as each brain cell dies at least one memory is set loose and it sparks for just a moment like a little shock shooting through the brain. And I think the last thing you remember before dying is being born. I've never had anyone to tell my theory to. If I told Helen she'd say I was nuts.

Mrs. Dipardi didn't answer me. For a moment she moved her eyes and was going to speak, but she didn't. I puffed up her pillows on the side very gently, hoping it would make her more comfortable. Then I checked the oxygen flow and the tubes to make sure they weren't pressing too hard against her nose.

"Do you need anything?" I asked again.

Still there was no answer. I decided to go back in the bathroom and check out Lloyd's hair brushes. My hair looked thinner and more mousy brown than usual because it was still wet, so I rubbed my head with a towel. Suddenly I heard a strange voice coming from the direction of Lloyd's room.

"Are you Binky?"

I stopped rubbing my head with the towel and thought I had imagined the weird little voice. I

91

moved to the bedroom door and looked in and there was Mrs. Dipardi, with her head turned looking right at me.

"Are you Binky?" she asked again.

A chill ran through me for some reason, and I took my time folding up the towel before going into the bedroom. Her voice had sounded like it belonged to a ventriloquist's dummy. Most of her features still looked sweet, but the pathetic red eyes set against her chalk-white face and hair made her look like a porcelain statuette. Now, a second later, there was something mildly horrifying about a tiny smile on her face.

I decided I probably didn't hear right. She probably hadn't said what I thought she said. It must have just sounded like it. She probably just wanted a glass of water or a Kleenex. I moved slowly into the bedroom and Carmelita moved her head, keeping her eyes hooked on me. I stopped at the bottom of her bed and felt relieved that from this position she looked much more normal with her head set straight on her body even though she was still looking at me.

"Did you say something?" I inquired.

She waited a moment, and then that funny voice came again. Her lips parted and she asked quite clearly, "Where is Lloyd's little Binky Bear?"

I decided the morphine was probably confusing her. Sometimes it does that just before putting a patient to sleep. I also decided that maybe all she wanted was someone in the room while she drifted off to sleep, so I sat down in the overstuffed chair near the gym equipment in the corner. We sort of looked at each other for a couple of minutes. Then her eye-lids fluttered and finally closed. A second later they sprang open and she let out a moan.

"Are you all right?" I wanted to know.

"Oh, yes, just thinking," she said weakly.

"Would you like something?" I asked her.

"Please . . . prop up my pillows . . . dear," she responded.

"Sure," I said.

Before I knew what was happening, her arms were curling up around my neck like snakes and her head slowly lifted itself toward mine. Her eyes were coming closer, her face closer. I thought it was an attempt to gain greater support, that she was summoning every bit of strength just to lift her bones. But then her head suddenly veered and I felt a terrible pain in my left arm. At first I thought I had strained a muscle, but I looked down and saw Mrs. Dipardi's teeth clamped onto my skin like a vise. It was as if I was being pulled into a coffin by a vampire and I pulled away and let out a good yell. I was bleeding, and I ran into the bathroom and shoved my arm under the cold-water tap. I yelled a couple of more times, and I was really shocked to see the outline of her teeth on my skin. I was so confused I tried to keep my one arm under the water faucet while rummaging through Lloyd's medicine cabinet with the other. I didn't know what I was doing. I probably thought I would find some bottle that said HUMAN BITE OINTMENT. Finally, I saw some Unguentine spray, so I let a blast of it hit the wound and I let out a couple of more yells and groans. I kept running between the water faucet and the medicine cabinet, and then looking into the bedroom. There she was, poor Carmelita, sitting up staring at me with a big smile on her face.

10

"ANYBODY HERE?"

I was still in a state of shock when I heard the voice. "In here," I called out. "In the bathroom!" A moment later Rosemary was in the doorway.

"What happened?"

"She bit me!" I howled. "She bit me!" I pointed to the red marks on my arm.

Rosemary had some kind of item from the dry cleaners on a hanger which she threw onto the doorknob and hurried to my side. She grabbed a washcloth, ran it under the cold water, and pressed it against the spot. "That's not so bad," she observed. "Didn't Lloyd warn you she was a biter?"

"No," I moaned.

"Where is your mother?" Rosemary asked.

"On a Chop Suey break."

Rosemary bolted into action. "I'll take care of it."

She went into the bedroom to see if Carmelita was all right and Carmelita tried to bite her, too. It didn't take me long to see Rosemary was an old hand at foiling hostile choppers. I couldn't hear everything she was saying to the old lady on account of the water was running in the sink, but it must have been all the right things because after a few more lunges Carmelita looked like a sweet, sedate woman again.

I staggered out into the living room. Now I really smelled of antiseptic and I thought I had frostbite of the arm. I even chugalugged a can of Schaefer hoping it would cut the pain. Then I started pacing nervously.

"She's asleep now," Rosemary said when she finally tiptoed into the living room with her plastic drycleaning bag. She made certain all the doors to Lloyd's bedroom were securely closed, and let out a big sigh. "Whew," she said, grabbing herself a beer and sitting on the sofa. She straightened out the dry-cleaning bag on her lap.

"Sit over here," Rosemary urged, patting the sofa. A little puff of dust rose up. "Come on," Rosemary insisted.

I took my can of Unguentine spray with me and sat down. She moved over next to me and gently felt around the bite marks. Her touch made me feel so good I knew she would make a wonderful nurse if she wanted to be one.

"Do you think she has rabies?" I asked.

"No," Rosemary assured me. "This isn't even going to need a tetanus shot. The worst you'll get is a teensie infection."

"Oh, great."

Her hands stayed on my arm and she seemed to really feel sorry for me. I reached out and took one of her hands in mine and she smiled. Then she started giving me a back massage and I realized she had a few medical theories of her own. "This'll really get the blood moving. Speed the white blood corpuscles up to the arm," she laughed.

"No kidding," I mumbled, and I felt so close to her I was even going to tell her my brain-cell theory right there and then but I didn't.

"I'm not kidding," she said emphatically. "Those WC's get in there like angry parameciums and eat up all the germs. I learned something in bio, you know."

"What's that on the hanger?" I asked.

"Her favorite dress," Rosemary replied matter-of-factly. "Carmelita asked me to get it cleaned before she went into the hospital. It's very pretty." Rosemary got up and tore the plastic covering off. It looked like an old-fashioned white lace gown.

"It's real nice," I said.

"It was her wedding dress!" Rosemary took it off the hanger and held it up in front of her. "Attractive, eh?"

"Oh, yes."

"I'll put it on and you'll get a better idea."

"Do you think you should?"

"Sure," she said. "I won't model it in where she can see it. She broke down crying when she asked me to clean it because she said she and the old man danced for hours at Shoal's Lobster Restaurant the night they got married and the band played 'Come Back to Sorrento' four times."

As Rosemary talked she stood up and slipped out of her jeans and blouse. I made believe that sort of thing was run-of-the-mill in my life and started humming and spraying Unguentine on my arm.

"See!" she announced proudly, walking right to the middle of the living room and doing a couple of turns. She looked very, very nifty. Her big eyes and long black hair really looked great against all the white lace.

"Does the bite still hurt?" she pursued, sitting next to me and starting to rub my back again.

"No."

"You look very sad," she observed.

"Did Harold tell you all the things Lloyd said to me this morning?" I wanted to know.

"I had a beer with them down at the Maypole," she said. "Lloyd's half loaded already, along with Bob and that crazy Greek girl—they're trying to get a party together for tonight, so I left. Even Harold's drinking —and he told me Lloyd really put you through the wringer."

"He despises me, if that's what you mean," I said.

"No, he doesn't," she disagreed. "Hasn't he adopted you yet?" she asked directly.

I looked at her and thought I must have misunderstood her question. "What?"

"*Adopted* you. Taken you under his wing," she repeated.

"No, of course not. Why would he take me under his wing if he hates me?" I asked her.

She began to rub farther down my back, which I

suppose was intended to get some of the lower corpus-cles to rise to the occasion.

"Oh that feels good," I said.

"I can tell he likes you," Rosemary remarked.

"Well he's got a strange way of showing it," I said.

"Lloyd can be critical," Rosemary agreed, "but he's shaping you up. He shapes all of us up."

"I can use some shaping up," I admitted. "But you! What could he possibly want to improve about you?" I asked, puzzled.

"Lloyd thought I should be more feminine," Rosemary said, "like wearing softer makeup. And he also told me how a man likes to be treated. For example, he told me to always carry Winston cigarettes in my pocketbook, just in case my date wants a cigarette and runs out."

"That's stupid," I said. "Why should you be the cigarette supplier?"

"I tried it a few times, then began resenting buying cigarettes that only Lloyd would ask for. He also wanted to change the kind of clothes I wear. He wanted me to look more sophisticated and then I realized he wanted me to look better to use me as bait," she confessed.

"Bait?" I asked. "What kind of bait?"

"Lloyd's got something for kids," Rosemary revealed. "Maybe because he wants to be young again. Maybe because he still thinks he's a kid, deep down. Like sometimes he takes five or six kids and me out fishing to Sandy Hook in this boat he's got. The kids usually get permission to come along because they tell their parents I'm going and their parents like me."

"Why doesn't he like people his own age?" I asked her.

"It's what Carmelita did to him when he was very young. She really hurt him," Rosemary told me.

"Does what Carmelita did have anything to do with a bear?" I asked, the thought leaping into my mind.

"How did you know?"

"Before she nibbled my arm she asked something about a *Binky Bear*," I told her, trying to remember exactly what that weird voice did say.

Rosemary moved closer to me and I could feel my whole side grow warm.

"Lloyd tells the story a little differently, depending on how drunk he is," she explained, starting to massage my elbows. "When he was three years old Carmelita saw him doing something with a toy bear."

"What?"

"I don't know exactly what," she confessed, "but it was more serious than kissing. It was just a regular stuffed animal that belonged to some girl cousin of his who was also about three years old at the time and she told Lloyd to do something to it. I mean, it wasn't really supposed to be dirty. It was like two kids playing doctor with a Barbie doll, then he started examining his cousin. I mean, there's healthy exploration like that going on in any prekindergarten class in any school any day of the week, but Carmelita caught Lloyd and dragged him to the kitchen oven and lit a match and said he was a horrid filthy three-year-old and she was going to burn off all the sinful parts of his anatomy. And that's the only thing Lloyd really re-

members about being a kid, which is a pretty horrendous thing!"

"It is!" was all I could say, but I felt a great swell of
pity for any kid who had to go through a thing like
that.

"Anyway that twisted Lloyd's mind," she said, "and
because of that, he wants to prove what a man he is
with us kids. Lloyd's got a lot to give, but he wants
what he wants and he gets it by charm or by money. Lloyd feels everyone's got a price," Rosemary explained. "Five dollars is a lot to kids around this
town."

For a few moments I felt very ashamed because
even as she was explaining the terrible thing Carmelita had done to Lloyd as a kid, I found myself almost
desperately thinking about my own life. About Rosemary. I mean, I really felt as though I were falling in
love with her. I wanted to marry her. My mind was
really getting ahead of itself, to say the least. I wanted
to have kids with her, and to live with her and maybe
we'd even have twins and we'd give them so much
love they'd be the happiest kids in the world. I know
that sounds crazy but you do hear stories of love at
first sight and I really thought this might be one of
them.

"Does it feel good?" she asked, her fingers roaming
around my neck like crazy.

"Terrific."

"I don't usually bother telling anybody about Lloyd
and what goes on here because it sounds preposter-
ous, but I don't think Lloyd is the only one. I'll bet
there's somebody like him in every town. God knows

there's a willing audience. Kids who can't wait to get out of their houses and go someplace to drink and smoke without a hassle. Especially for free. It's like a secret thing that happens and the kids usually never tell other kids or priests or anybody because they're so ashamed or suffer amnesia after the fact. I tried to tell my father when I first found out about Lloyd but he didn't believe me. It's like only the kids know what really goes on here. My father just thinks I have a vivid imagination."

Then for the first time that night I really looked into her gorgeous eyes and she looked back into mine.

"You're a very sensitive person," I said. "I never met anyone like you before on Staten Island." Rosemary put her arm around me and gave me a big hug. She just sat there, her lips real rosy, and I smelled her gardenia cologne. I leaned toward her and kissed her —and she kissed me back! The kiss took my breath away and I just sat there floating.

"You're very nice," she said to me. I couldn't even answer her but I know she could hear my heart going a mile a minute.

"Do you know, the first thing Lloyd ever told me when he was stewed was that he wanted to commit suicide," she said, resting her head on my shoulder. I could see reflections of light bouncing off her silky black hair as I moved my fingers through it.

"See, whatever Lloyd does, he doesn't want to hurt anyone. In many ways he's a teddy bear. What he really wants is to have people around him, and it's only teenagers who can stand him," Rosemary continued. "When I first met him he wasn't as bad. Now his liver is giving out from all the bourbon. He has arthritis in his knees and fingers. Everything is going wrong. He's cracking up, I think. You haven't seen him go downhill. What you're seeing is Custer's Last Stand, because he loves his mother and he also hates her for what she did to him as a kid. She made sure her son could never totally love another person."

"That must be the worst thing that can happen to a human being," I said quietly, and I couldn't help thinking of Helen. It really depressed me to think of how much love there might have been in my family and with my father if only we had been normal and Dad and Helen had really loved each other. For some reason I felt afraid at that moment, but I didn't want Rosemary to see it so I looked away, but then I really reached out for her and we just sat on the sofa with our arms around each other.

"The day they took Carmelita to the hospital Lloyd lost his power of speech," Rosemary said sadly. "His vocal chords gave out. When they gave her a spinal tap, he broke down crying."

"If he has such strong feelings for his mother, why does he have noisy kids coming over so much?" I asked her.

"To be truthful, I think it's to stop him from thinking about how much he hates God," Rosemary said. "And if he wants a party, I can't stop him. I'd rather he plan a party than hear him talk about putting a bullet through his brain," she told me.

"Does he have a gun?" I asked.

"He says he does, but we have no way of knowing. Harold searched his room but couldn't find one," Rosemary said with concern.

Suddenly there was the sound of a car turning into the driveway and screeching to a halt.

"Who's that?" I jolted forward.

"Probably the King," Rosemary said, straightening the dress.

11

LLOYD WAS ALONE AND SO DRUNK HE HAD TO CONCEN-trate very hard just to do one thing at a time—like walk. It all looked very mechanical the way he was using every drop of his attention to walk a straight line into the living room. There's nothing more in-credible than watching a drunk make believe he isn't drunk.

"Where's Harold and Bob?" Rosemary asked.

Lloyd strained to look at us standing in front of the couch. He observed our outfits like he was studying the appearance of mannequins in a costume museum. Without saying a word he then switched his atten-tion to getting his body to use the tallboy and pouring himself a water glass full of Wild Turkey.

"Are the kids still coming?" Rosemary wanted to know.

"They ran out of gas, but they'll be here!" he said.

"They're probably on the road already, so don't worry, the party always begins at midnight." Then he started laughing.

"Why didn't Harold come home with you?" I wanted to know.

"Because I told him and Bob to have another brew, that's why," Lloyd explained. He could see Rosemary and I were suspicious so he added: "I figured it was better to assign him *and* Bob to make sure those kids get here because two retards are better than one, don't you agree?"

Rosemary and I both stood alert as Lloyd turned the knob to open the bedroom door. We could hear the oxygen bubbling from the tanks within like noises in an aquarium.

"Oh, by the way," he said, pausing and shooting his full gaze on Rosemary, before fully opening the door, "get out of my mother's dress."

Lloyd opened the door and stopped dead at the sight of Carmelita in his bed. We didn't know what he was going to do. He just stood quietly in the doorway for about a full minute looking at his pathetic old mother, and then came back into the living room, closing the door gently behind him.

"Who put her in there?" he asked.

"My mother," I said.

"Where is she?"

"She told you she needed a break," I reminded him.

"Well, that was very thoughtful," he said, taking a big drink of the bourbon. "In fact, that was so thoughtful I want you to take a ride with me."

I looked at him as though his mind must have

slipped Beyond the Planet of the Grapes. "I wouldn't take a ride with you for a million bucks," I said nervously.

"You wouldn't?" he said with amazement.

"Why do you want him to take a ride with you?" Rosemary inquired.

"There's a storm due tonight. Small-craft warnings. I've got to go down to the marina and make sure my boat's tied up straight. Weigh it down with a little water," he answered rather sensibly.

"*I'll* go with you," Rosemary suggested.

"No. I want *him*," Lloyd said strongly, with a flash of the old shark eyes. "See, Chris, I need a man to do a man's work. I might need a little muscle," he added sarcastically.

I said right off, "Forget it."

Lloyd gave me a smile, turned quickly, and bounded up the attic stairs like a kangaroo.

"Is he nuts?" I asked.

Rosemary gave me a signal to keep quiet as she went toward the stairs. She hardly got three steps before Lloyd came bounding back down with something. He literally ran through the living room and kitchen outside to his car. It all happened so quickly, but a moment later I realized he had my father's coat under his arm. It still took me another moment to react. "He's got my father's coat!" I cried out. "He's got my father's coat!" By now my puzzlement had changed to rage and I ran out of the house after him. "You give me back that coat," I screamed at him as I arrived just in time to see him throw the chesterfield into the trunk of the yellow Ford and slam it shut.

Lloyd laughed and started to get into the car. I ran at him and tried to grab the keys out of his hand, but he just threw me to the ground. In a flash he had the doors locked, the windows rolled up, and the motor running. I started kicking the car door and yelling, "Give me my coat! Give me my coat!" I could see Lloyd laughing behind the wheel as he slipped the trunk key off the key ring and stuck it in his left pocket. Rosemary was telling me something, but I was so confused I couldn't listen. Action was the only thing on my mind so I instinctively ran and grabbed a big rock and came galloping at the car. I was all set to smash in the windshield when Lloyd rolled down the driver's window about three inches.

"You want your daddy's coat back?" he laughed.

I held the rock poised high in the air. "Give me it!" I shouted.

Lloyd stopped laughing and then he sounded like he was trying to plea bargain, but I didn't believe him at all. "Look, all I'm asking is a little favor. I can't tie the boat alone. It takes two people and it's better if Rosemary stays with my mother, okay? Come on, please?" he added, and he seemed suddenly cold sober.

"Go with him," Rosemary said, and I could tell she had carefully sized up the situation before speaking. "He won't hurt you," she said deliberately right in front of Lloyd.

Lloyd looked insulted. "Of course, I won't." He lowered his window all the way. "Come on, Chris, please. It'll just take a few minutes. I'll give you the coat back, I promise. I can't let anything happen to the boat because I need to sell it!"

I really didn't know what I was doing, but I put that rock down and Rosemary led me around to the other side of the car. She gave me a little kiss on the cheek which made me think she knew no harm would come to me. I trusted her, and as the car backed out of the driveway the headlights picked her up in the old white wedding dress she was still wearing and I felt as though she were too good to be true. Of course that's how I feel whenever something beautiful comes even near my life.

It was about a two-mile drive down to the Oakwood Kills marina, but the way Lloyd drove from side to side on the road I knew he hadn't sobered up and it ended up being about four miles. It was the longest-shortest drive of my life and Lloyd seemed to have his eyes glued on the road and to have totally forgotten I was even in the car. And one thing he was right about when he had been yelling at his insurance agent was that that pin-striped Ford sure did need a valve job. There was a tap-tap-tapping in the engine that sounded like thirty midget teenagers were in the crankcase trying to escape. Then, on top of that, with Lloyd behind the wheel it was like riding The Wild Mouse, and what took the cake was there was this mysterious, heavy, round white object on the seat between us. I was afraid to focus on it at first because I wanted to keep my eye on the road in case Lloyd started driving through a house or something. But this white thing was about a foot in diameter and seemed to be some kind of stone. Actually, it looked like a grinder's wheel that a person would use to sharpen knives and other sundry cutlery.

"What is this?" I finally asked.

"A salt block," Lloyd said.

I reached my hand over to it and sure enough, it felt exactly like a salt block. I wet a finger and gave it a rub and a taste and that was proof positive.

"There I was, sitting at that bar making phone calls —trying to get a good party together—and trying to get the insurance company to pay for the valve job on this lemon," Lloyd explained, "and then everything fell into place. I thought of the salt block and how my five-hundred-dollar deductible clause would soon be taken care of."

"What's the salt block got to do with your insurance policy?"

"You'll find out," he said, brimming with vengeance over the thought of that insurance agent Rocco.

I just kept my mouth shut until we reached the marina. It was as deserted and spooky as a graveyard, and Lloyd had to get out and open a lock on a fence and then we drove into this place that looked like the spot where ships go to die. There was a full moon and everybody knows that's when all the loony people go even loonier. It seemed to me Lloyd was accelerating too fast in the marina parking lot and before I knew what was happening we were racing toward the water.

"Hey," I yelled as the car sped forward. I sat high in my seat and could see a cement launching ramp right in front of us and I was going to let out a scream.

In a split second I worked it out in my mind that I'd grab the door handle and try to throw myself clear if he didn't stop. I even had the vision of not being able to get out of the car and sinking with it but finding an air bubble in the roof and being able to stay alive until divers reached me. If you ever want to feel really mixed up, try worrying about saving your deceased father's coat, your semiworthless life, and your precious sanity from a psychopathic shipyard worker all within two seconds.

12

LLOYD BROUGHT THE CAR TO A SCREECHING HALT AT the very edge of the boat launching ramp. I took a deep gulp of sea air and my heart felt like it was performing kamikaze dives against my rib cage. Lloyd looked calm, cool, and loaded as he got out and swayed his way around to the rear of the car. I thought he was going to open the trunk and present me with my father's coat, but instead he hoisted himself up on the back of the car. He lit a cigarette and from his perch on the roof he seemed to be enjoying my fright over the near plunge into the water. By now I was angry.

"Where's the boat?" I demanded to know.

"*There*," he answered, waving a finger in three directions.

"Where?"

"What's the matter, are you blind?" he inquired, steadying his hand and pointing at this big junky thing that was out of the water and up on wooden mounts. It looked like a stranded ghost ship in the moonlight and it had a keel covered with barnacles.

"There's not going to be a storm, is there?" I asked rhetorically. I didn't need an answer.

"You never can tell," Lloyd said, his eyes glowing like those of an animal about to leap from a tree.

I backed away, but then turned on him. "What'd you drag me down here for?"

Lloyd took a deep drag on his cigarette and blew a smoke ring at the moon. "I wanted to tell you I'm sorry."

"For what?" I wanted to know, and I kept my distance from the car in case he decided to pounce and start choking me.

"I'm sorry for the way I tore into you this morning. The way I hurt you."

"You didn't hurt me," I stated as I felt all the pain coming back. How I could say that when he had seen me crying was beyond me. The truth was I could still feel Lloyd grabbing me by the shoulders and slamming me against his bedroom door. *You take care of your body. You respect yourself. Wipe those crumbs off your face. We don't drink out of milk cartons around here.*

"You can't hurt me," I said.

Lloyd's gaze turned slowly from the stars and shone down on my face like Satan.

"How come you're so spiffy now?" Lloyd asked.

"I'm not spiffy."

114

"You smell like you gargled with Old Spice."

"Look, Mr. Dipardi," I said, deciding to be very formal, "I just want my father's coat back and then I'll get out of here and you can torment horseshoe crabs or whatever you're into for the evening."

"Has Rosemary been giving me bad press?" Lloyd asked. "She can't be trusted, you know."

"Don't talk about her like that."

"Look, I like Rosemary," Lloyd said. "She's a sweet, wonderful, considerate budding concubine."

"She is not a budding concubine, she's a wonderful girl and talk about her with respect," I told him.

He looked up at the sky and blew another smoke ring.

There was a pause, then Lloyd finally spoke. "Chris, I underestimated you," he said finally. He sounded like he was playing cat and mouse and I was the mouse.

"Great. Now give me back my father's coat."

"But I also wanted you to know why I was as cruel as I was."

"Don't bother."

"I insist," he said.

"Why don't you just save that confession for your social worker or parole officer, whichever gets you first?" I suggested.

"Chris, the reason I was so mean to you was because you remind me of *me*." Lloyd seemed to be savoring his words now. I mean, just the way he spoke now I could tell he really had read a lot of those books at his house. People who read books always use words differently.

"I don't know what you're talking about," I confessed.

"What I'm saying is that maybe the reason I'm so demanding of you is because you remind me of *me* when I was your age. Half developed. Half conscious. And half a man." He really glared at me now. "And that means you only have half your work done. Take a look at me. I'm twice your age and where has it gotten me? My life is no better than it was when I was fifteen. And kid, I don't want to see you make the same mistakes I did," he said, almost meekly. "I know what it's like to have a witch for a mother. And just because my father was around physically doesn't mean I had a father any more than you do. I really feel for you, kid, and I don't want to see you grow up twisted."

"I'm not twisted!" I screamed at him. "Don't call me that."

"Are you kidding? Face the truth," he said, his voice strong again. "No matter what school you ever went to, I'd bet all you ever got called was Mama's boy."

"Is this what you brought me out here for? Is it?" I asked. I hated myself for beginning to shake and lose my composure.

"Yes," he said matter-of-factly. I couldn't move. Finally I turned and started walking away, back toward the exit. I stopped in my tracks when Lloyd banged his foot on the roof of the car. It sounded like a shot. In a chilling whisper, he said, "One of these days your dead father will let go of you, and you'll be free. No more a slave to a dream which can never come true. Then, kid, it's up to you. You can cut the power line your mother has plugged into you, and stop blaming her for your failures. Start accepting the responsibility for your own life and then you can be a man."

I turned to him and cried out: "What do you know about being a man!" I felt an urge to really sock him one.

Lloyd flexed his muscles. "Look. I joined a gym. I put inches on my arm. I brought my voice down an octave! I even put a mirror in front of the telephone so I could study my expressions. I did everything I could to present myself as a man." Then he roared, banging his foot on the roof of the car again. *"Lloyd, the toughest man in town! 'King of the Kids!' Lloyd the Great still looking for Pop-Goes-the-Hero.* The outside looked *terrific,* but inside—forget it. What I didn't know was the change had to come from the inside first. I started the wrong way."

I thought for a moment he was going to fly up into the moonlight like a winged centaur, but then his energy waned and he sat back down. He looked straight into my eyes, but this time with what seemed like kindness. After a few moments his lips opened and a strained voice came out. "Then when the day comes and you're too old for Pop-Goes-the-Hero anymore, you decide to *be* just Pop. Do you get what I'm saying? You can become anything you want. You can be a Hero. All you have to do is have the vision and then grab hold of it so tight and don't let go until you have it in your hot little hands. Aim for the moon, kid. Don't end up like me."

"I feel very sorry for you," I said softly.

"And, Chris, my boy, I also feel sorry for me. I wish

I was dead." He smiled like a sad clown and lowered himself down off the car. He stared at me a moment longer and then reached into his pocket and came up with the trunk key. He unlocked the trunk, picked up my father's coat, held it a moment, and then tossed it to me. Then he got into the car and slammed the door. I wasn't going to let him leave without me so I ran to the right front seat and got back in, holding the coat on my lap.

"Can I have a lift back?" I asked.

"No," he said, starting the engine.

I figured he had misunderstood me and I turned to him to explain that all I wanted was a ride back to the house, when I noticed him lifting the salt block from the front seat and putting it on the floor of the car. He rammed it smack against the accelerator. The motor roared and the tapping of the valves became a deafening noise as though the pistons were going to explode through the engine block. "I hate this town and this world! I also hate insurance agents! Get out!" he yelled at me, and he didn't have to yell twice. I jumped clear of the car without even a chance to close the door as he threw the gearshift into forward. He leaped out of the car just as the wheels spun a cloud of dirt into the air. In a second the wheels were on the cement launching ramp and it was the first time I had ever seen a brand-new yellow pin-striped Ford drive itself into the ocean.

13

I FLED THE BOATYARD AND MADE A SHARP RIGHT SO THIS large wooden building would block Lloyd from seeing where I went. About three hundred yards down the street, my left foot plopped into a big puddle so I selected a spot behind a hedge in the front yard of somebody's house. I crouched to watch Lloyd come out of the marina gate and lock it up again. He looked up and down the street and then meandered back up the street in the direction of his house. When he was out of sight I lay back on the grass and was thankful I hadn't picked a yard with a Doberman pinscher waiting to attack me. It was just one of those beach bungalows with a tiny Virgin Mary grotto on the side. I had a pain in my head as though my brain was expanding, and my heart hurt so much I thought I was on the verge of having a teenage thrombosis. It took me about ten minutes before I had the strength to hobble back out onto the street and head for the corner where Lloyd had disappeared. When I got to the corner I could see him about three blocks up Hillside Terrace swaying his way forward under a streetlight and I was grateful because as long as I kept him in my sight I didn't have to worry about him leaping out from behind some bush to hack me to death.

I followed him all the way up to Hylan Boulevard. He kept going but I stopped short because I saw this big black cat sitting in the middle of the highway and it was staring at me. It was a very freaky sight but that's the way my life is. I can just walk along a street minding my own business and I'll come across things like a lady sitting on a curb breast-feeding a baby or a man rubbing the back of a hunchbacked girl or some poor guy talking to himself. In other parlance, wherever I go there is the unusual. Anyway, this time it was a black cat reclining in the middle of this busy boulevard and it was positioned so it looked like it had been half run over by a car, squashing part of its body into a type of base like a buttress for a paper doll. It looked like I was staring at a stone statue of a cat with metallic eyes glazed with fire and that if I wanted to I could just take the thing home and use it as a garden ornament. The animal seemed very dead except for its eyes, and I had the strangest feeling it might still be alive.

Well, needless to say I sprang into action. *Action Chris*, that's what they call me. I put my father's coat down on the curb and ran right out into the traffic and started flagging cars to make them slow down. I was almost run over four times before I reached the cen-

terline of the boulevard and inspected the cat at close
range. The amazing thing was that the cat looked in
perfect condition but absolutely stiff. I decided that
even though its eyes were frozen open the poor thing
had to be dead. It was probably hit by a bumper, and
just happened to land in a natural-looking position.
Whatever, I felt it would be wrong to leave the thing
there because at any moment some car would veer
over the centerline. It seemed like letting that happen
would be an offense against both nature and the sani-
tation department. I didn't know what to do except
flag cars coming from both directions to keep them
from plowing into me or the cat, but then I saw a big
piece of cardboard in a gutter a little way up the
street. The traffic slowed a bit so I ran and got the
cardboard and put it down next to the cat. With my
right foot I gently rolled the cat onto the cardboard
and it still looked dead except for those eyes. There
wasn't a twitch out of it as I pulled the whole ca-
boodle over to the gutter and just missed getting
clipped by an oil truck. I really didn't know what to
do then, so I sat down on the curb and contemplated
the situation. I figured I could run up to a house, ring
the bell, and ask to call the ASPCA. Then I figured if
I told the ASPCA the feline looked dead already
they'd probably just tell me to put it in a Glad bag
and leave it in a garbage can. Then I thought about
burying it, but there was still something very freaky
about those eyes. Finally I picked up a stick and gave
the cat a gentle poke. Well, I want to tell you I almost
dropped dead when that cat sprang straight up in the
air, its momentum hurling the cardboard in my face,

and flew out of the gutter to disappear into a vacant lot. I was certain I had witnessed a supernatural event as I retrieved my dad's coat and cleared out quick. In fact, I ran for at least three blocks up this street called Norton's Lane until I could see Lloyd again. He was far ahead but at least it was another human being.

I couldn't take my mind off the cat and after a while I began to pat myself on the back that I had performed a magnificent resuscitation rescue. "I saved a pussycat," I kept repeating to myself. "I saved a pussycat." Sometime if you ever feel your life isn't worth a plug nickel try saving a cat. It does wonders.

Lloyd turned up Oakwood Kills Lane and by that time I knew where I was. I took my time and let Lloyd get way ahead because I really didn't know what I was going to do when I got to the house. Now there were two thoughts running through my head. One was about Rosemary. I took my sweet time thinking of Rosemary and how wonderful she was. Lloyd might tell her about me when he got back to the house. He could make up all kinds of stories and really try to turn her against me. From here on in, this confession gets very truthful so I have to write down these things very fast no matter how much it hurts me. It's true that kids always called me names no matter where I lived, and no matter where I went to school. The worst name I was ever called was when I was eleven years old and went to P.S. 8. I was called CBRH because I started crying one day when a kid hit me in my eye with a pencil. Do you have any idea what it's like to be only eleven years old and have your schoolmates calling you CBRH all the time?

They'd call me it in class. They'd call me it on the streets. They'd make anonymous phone calls and ask my mother if they could talk to CBRH. It was horrible. The entire school knew that CBRH stood for "CRY-BABY ROOSTER HEAD." It was the most horrendous thing that ever happened to me because they could call me *CBRH* anywhere and get away with it. If a teacher or my mother wasn't around they'd say the whole thing: "CRY-BABY ROOSTER HEAD! CRY-BABY ROOSTER HEAD!" They'd sing it like "Lizzie Borden took an ax and gave her father forty whacks!"

As I walked under the full moon something that made me really worried was how Lloyd seemed to know exactly what I'd been through. It seemed he knew precisely how to hurt me. I felt like I was in this painting I once saw where a guy is on a raft and sharks are circling. Maybe there *was* something wrong with me.

When I turned the corner at Half Moon Street I heard a party going on and I didn't have to wonder where it was. It was all that Greek dance music blasting away again. Lloyd must have gotten back to the house at least a half hour ahead of me, because I also stopped outside one house and petted a Saint Bernard for twenty minutes. You very rarely get a chance to pet a Saint Bernard so I figured I'd better take advantage of the opportunity at the time. Also, I guess I needed somebody very badly just to snuggle up against and make me feel like a human being even if this particular somebody turned out to be a drooler.

I finally walked up the driveway and let me tell

you, Lloyd's impromptu social function was in full swing and rather startling right off the bat. The first thing was this Bonneville convertible with a heart-shaped plastic rear window. I hadn't seen a heart-shaped plastic rear window in years and it sort of gave me a clue to Lloyd's guest list. I didn't have the strength to just rush right in and say, "Hi, everybody, my name's Chris," so I stood out in the driveway awhile.

Then I strolled around outside for a few minutes to get the lay of the land. Some kids were rolling around on the grass but the main outdoor action was taking place around the suburban pool. I didn't talk to anybody because they all looked so drunk or in other states of ecstasy that they didn't even seem to notice me. I felt like I was just a visiting zombie over from the Isle of the Dead. When I don't know kids I just make up names for them so I can keep them straight in my mind, and then if I get introduced I try to remember their real names, but I usually can't. I went to one party when I was at New Dorp at which I only knew the host so I gave everybody numbers. Anyway, some of the names I made up for the kids playing around Lloyd's pool were Bert the Bird (because he looked like a grosbeak), Susan the Hippo, Eddie Birthmark, Bobby the Babylonian, and Joe Lunatic. Susan the Hippo looked like she weighed three hundred teenage pounds and should have the titular lead in a movie called *My Summer at Carvel's*.

When I saw the dimensions of the out-of-doors fete I became intrigued with what must be going on inside the house. The screen door was flying open and closed like the flap on a chicken coop. Kids were commuting back and forth with beer cans and glasses of booze, and jumping up and down to the music. I felt really awful because all this noise wasn't the best thing for Carmelita's sleep. I was also worried about Helen because Rosemary might have had to tell her where I had gone. Then I got a look at what was going on in the kitchen and living room and my concern over Rosemary was intensified. The main motif was a row of what looked like rough Greek dancing kids. Bob and Quily were in the middle leading like crazy with flowerpots on their heads, and they had their arms around these tough Greco dancers I hadn't seen before. Just looking at them you knew that among them they couldn't form one complete sentence. One of the kids I nicknamed Apollo because he looked like the largest, most happy-go-lucky boy I had ever seen except on the silver screen. Then there was another Greek I called Zorba the Sneak because he looked villainous and kept singing "La la—la la la la la." I tried to slip insignificantly through the living room as Quily did a triple turn and all the kids said "*Hooray!*" I don't think the architecture of Lloyd's bungalow was intended for so many thundering squats and foot stampings because occasionally some flakes of plaster would fall from the ceiling. In fact, between the thumping and the bass sounds emanating from the speakers it seemed like an earthquake was in process. I got panicky over Rosemary because I didn't see her. Another girl in the chorus line was this one with a generous platinum wig and a face painted up like she had been imported direct from Times Square where you'd expect to see her waving at you from a doorway. Just as I tried to squeeze by she slipped and fell on the floor. Everybody laughed and the kids helped pick her up. Bob was right there, too, gentleman that he was.

"Where's Rosemary?" I asked him over the din. I was really frightened for her now that I saw how demented some of the kids were.

"Hey, Chris!" Bob said.

"Where's Rosemary?" I repeated.

Bob helped lift the platinum-wigged girl into a standing position and introduced me before her head was erect.

"This is Rosemary's sister, Dolly," he said, indicating the mass of platinum and silver. "Dolly, say hello to Chris!"

Dolly threw her head upward like being called to attention. This girl had a face that looked like a thousand fanatical Avon ladies had been told to do a rouge-and-powder overkill. I couldn't believe this writhing intemperance could be even remotely related to Rosemary.

"Hello, honey," the girl wheezed.

"Where's Rosemary?" I asked.

"Honey, what are you doing with a winter coat?" her ruby lips asked.

I looked down at my arm and realized I had forgotten I was still clutching my father's coat, but it didn't matter because Dolly didn't wait for an answer but began dancing crazy again along with everybody else. I shoved my way to the attic stairs and ran up. First things first, I decided, hanging the chesterfield back up on the rafter near the window. At least the coat would be safe and then I could go find Rosemary. I was also worried about Harold, because I realized I hadn't seen him around either.

I ran back downstairs and noticed the door to the bathroom was ajar and I could hear Lloyd singing at the top of his lungs, "I've got a date with an angel! Got a date with a real live girl!" It was so freaky to hear the roar of the party in the front room, the screaming laughter from the pool, the stomping of feet all over—and then, out in the bathroom, this loaded, loud voice of the host of the party singing "I've got a date with an angel!"

The thought crossed my mind that maybe Rosemary had retreated to the old man's room trying to comfort him from the frightening racket going on. I went down the hall and knocked on the door. I figured she had to be there or in cowering with my mother and Carmelita. I thought maybe the old man's stroke had affected his hearing so I opened the door. The old guy didn't see me but I saw him and he was sitting in a chair with his feet up laughing at an *All in the Family* rerun. There was no Rosemary. I closed the door and started back up the hall when suddenly the bathroom door swung all the way open and I was face to face with Lloyd again. He looked at me, but he was still singing "I've got a date with an angel! Got a date with a real live girl!" What shocked me most was that he had gotten all cleaned up and dressed and he hardly looked drunk anymore. I know this sounds stupid, but there was a moment then when he looked like he was actually fond of me. I couldn't figure him out. Finally he turned his back on me and marched into the party, so I suppose most of all he looked like he was a guy determined to have a good time. He leaped into the dancing horde and there were renewed Hellenic cries of celebration from Quily and the crowd at the appearance of their host.

I looked around the kitchen and living room one more time for Rosemary. Maybe she had gone to look for me. And maybe Harold wasn't there because he was just so ashamed about Lloyd's shenanigans that he went to play miniature golf or something until it would all be over. He certainly hadn't cooked anything, because by now the kids were raiding the cupboards. There were sights like ten kids tearing apart a box of Cheez-Its, and when somebody found half a Sara Lee cherry cheesecake it looked like a gold rush. I realized I couldn't avoid facing the music any longer so I went into the bathroom and knocked on the bedroom door. There was no answer so I opened it. Carmelita was lying back in the bed with her eyes closed and breathing rapidly. My mother was sitting in a chair staring at me and there was only the *blop-blop-blop* sound of the oxygen bubbles sliding upward through the water filter. I closed the door behind me. It was as though I had entered a tomb.

"Where have you been?" Helen asked, looking ready to explode.

"He took Dad's coat," I explained.

"You went with him?" she asked.

"I had to get Dad's coat back," I said simply.

"Are you crazy?" Helen yelled. I couldn't answer that one. Finally, Helen grunted and turned the oxygen flow up.

"Lloyd came in here," Helen said. "He was frightened. That sick freak is frightened when he has to look at her," she said, indicating Carmelita. "He despises her."

"But he loves her, too," I said.

"And he hates me," she said, sitting back down and keeping an eye on the old lady. "He washes and sings," Helen said, looking at me. "He's singing; did you hear him?"

"Yes."

"He came into the room singing away and I told him his mother could use some cheering up, and I needed a few minutes relief, and he said no, he couldn't stay now because he was having a party. Can you imagine that? Another party." Helen sat back in her chair. Behind her, on a shelf, was the automatic turntable for the stereo. A record finished and the next one fell into place. There was silence for a few seconds and then I could hear the music blast again out in the living room.

"He said he'd break my arm if I stopped the records," she said.

"Have you seen Rosemary?" I asked.

"I haven't left this room for over an hour," she replied. I couldn't tell whether she was leaving something out or just preoccupied with her next thought. "We have to get out, you understand that?" she said.

"What about Carmelita?" I asked.

"There's not much else I can do for her," Helen said, standing up—and I knew she intended for us to hit the trail again! The Ritz Hotel—here we come!

14

HELEN ORDERED ME TO WAIT IN THE HALL WHILE SHE
went up the attic stairs to get the suitcases and shopping bags. It was the first time she was actually walking off a job. I felt terrible about leaving Carmelita. I
didn't think she should be left alone. In fact, it made
me so angry I wanted to charge right into the living
room and grab Lloyd to shake some sense into him.
And I would have done it if I hadn't known he had
the strength of a bear. The meanest person in the
world doesn't have a jubilee the night his mother
might die. He just doesn't.

There was a great burst of Greek happy-time noises
coming from the living room as I moved to the end
of the hall to look in. Lloyd, Bob, Quily, and about
twenty kids were all in lines doing the same old dancing with their arms around each other's shoulders,
looking like strings of boozed-up demons. Half the

kids from the pool had run in to dance, and Susan the Hippo was laughing so loud she looked like a grotesque mechanical freak in front of a carnival fun house. One, two, three, *dip!* One, two, three, *dip!* They were chanting as they all turned into one big conga line. I couldn't take it any longer. All I knew was I wanted out, too. I pushed my way through the living room, keeping close to the far wall and away from the dancers. I began to think Rosemary had come back and had been looking for me all this time in the room. My head rotated like radar. As I got near the kitchen it dawned on me that if Rosemary was anywhere she'd probably be outside because she wouldn't be a part of the insanity going on in the house. She'd be outside looking for me, maybe even as worried about me as I was about her. I no sooner stepped into the kitchen area when I saw Rosemary's sister again.

"Where's Rosemary?" I asked her.

"Why?" Dolly inquired as she studied me this time.

"Because I want to find her," I said.

"Don't bother. You're not her type!" Dolly said, fluttering her huge artificial eyelashes and reaching out her right hand to grab the musclebound Apollo around his waist. She hung on to Apollo and brought him in close to her. "Rosemary likes boys like *this*, right, kid?" Dolly said, and then burst into loud vulgar laughter. Apollo joined in to put me down by also laughing like a goon. I tried to push by but Apollo swung his other arm around Quily and now I was facing a wall three bodies wide. I was ready to charge through them when I saw Helen plowing her way toward me with suitcases and shopping bags. I took one of the suitcases out of Helen's hands.

"What are they doing to you?" she asked.

"Forget it," I said.

Suddenly *Lloyd* joined the trio in blocking our path.

"Where do you think you're going?" Lloyd inquired of Helen.

"Out," she said, starting to push past. "And you'd better get someone else to stay in there with your mother!"

"I paid for a full week!" Lloyd complained.

"I'll send you a refund!" my mother shot back, and Dolly absolutely screamed with laughter.

Lloyd pushed the trio in on both of us. I noticed Helen's teeth grinding in the three seconds it took for her to react. She dropped her stuff and her right arm shot out, grabbing a frying pan out of the kitchen sink, and before Lloyd knew what hit him, she brought that utensil down on his head like an outsized hammer. The force of the blow made a loud *BAM!* and knocked him right to the floor—not that it split open his skull or anything like that. It must have been more of a surprise than anything else. Following that pugilistic success, Helen made a further enthusiastic motion which didn't need any translation for anybody. That frying pan whirled in a half circle in front of us, forcing Lloyd and the trio to leap good and clear. Just from a sheer culinary point of view I found it ironic that Harold entered through the porch door at just that moment.

"What'd you do that for?" Lloyd asked Helen, picking himself up and rubbing the top of his head. Helen held on tight to that frying pan as she fumbled with some of the shopping bags. Lloyd shifted uncomfortably with the wind temporarily out of his sails. "I just wanted to party," he said, motioning Harold over. I could tell Lloyd was embarrassed over having been hit on the head with a frying pan in front of his guests.

"Harold"—he started trying to cover the embarrassment he felt—"the guests are hungry. Did you get all the food?"

"No," Harold said.

Lloyd's eyes opened wide with disbelief. He was obviously even further embarrassed. "Harold, I gave you money to get cold cuts from Shutz's. Where are they?"

Harold looked down at the floor. "I didn't get any," he mumbled.

"We have guests!" Lloyd shouted, his embarrassment turning to anger.

Harold looked at Lloyd pleadingly. "Please send everybody home. Please, Lloyd?"

"At least somebody has a little sense in this house," Helen said, now fully reloaded with her junk. "Harold," she said good and loud, "don't do anything this drunk ever asks you anymore!"

Lloyd stiffened and I could almost feel the hair on his head bristle. Suddenly his hand went flying through the air and smacked Harold back and forth across the face about a half dozen times before Apollo and I could stop him. Harold's face was red and his body was trembling and I felt so helpless. I just didn't know what to do.

"Are you okay?" I asked Harold.

"I'm okay, Chris," he said—but then he turned and ran out of the house.

"You should be locked up," Helen said, leading the way out of the house. I wanted to run back and find Rosemary but there I was shlepping our suitcases and junk through the crowd and down the porch steps.

15

CERTAIN BUSES STOP RUNNING AT NIGHT AND ONE OF them was the 116 that goes along Norton's Lane and Oakwood Kills Lane, which meant Helen and I had to lug the suitcases and stuff down to Hylan Boulevard. We could get the 103 bus there and it would get us to Tompkinsville and the Ritz Hotel. I kept bellyaching about how worried I was about Rosemary and Harold and Carmelita—but my mother told me to just shut up. She thought Harold was lucky Lloyd finally showed his real colors.

We waited over twenty minutes for the bus and most of the time Helen spent showing me what she had succeeded in stealing from Lloyd: *four* jars of mushrooms, eight packages of Lipton soup, nine silver dollars, the bottle of Head & Shoulders, the aspirins, *and* the canned ham—plus some new acquisitions such as potato chips, a stapler, and an ornamental snail. She never once mentioned the fact that the stuff she had first stolen had been repossessed, and I guess it didn't bother her because all she did was take it all over again with interest.

The bus was empty except for us and the driver so I made Helen sit in a seat by herself with her stuff and I took the seat behind her with my suitcase right next to me. For the most part I kept my eyes on my reflection in the window. My hair jumped and swung every time we hit a bump. *So, we're on the trail again,* I thought to myself. *Onward to the next job. Forward to the next case, maybe the next one will be infant care. A nice normal baby with a really swell mother and father.*

"Why don't you say anything?" Helen finally asked.

"I'm just hoping Rosemary's all right," I said.

"She was a tramp," Helen commented.

"She was not," I countered, and I couldn't help wishing I had a father to talk over my feelings with. I had the feeling Helen would never like any girl I cared about. I just looked out the window as we passed this one wooded section that's got a long sweeping hillside with a bandstand and an orphanage. *It's probably better to be an orphan,* I thought. Life was really too confusing.

By the time we got to New Dorp I was really depressed and I opened my suitcase. I poked through my junk for a full minute before I realized what was missing.

"Where's Dad's coat?" I asked with instant fear.

"I left it there," Helen said calmly.

"You did *what?*"

"I deliberately left it," she repeated. "Don't you un-

138

derstand English? It was an old rag—as worthless as your rotten father."

For a full minute I was paralyzed with outrage. Then I slammed my suitcase shut and went running down the aisle toward the bus driver.

"Stop the bus! Stop the bus!" I yelled.

I scared the driver so much that he must have thought he had run over somebody. He jammed on the brakes and I flew forward, banging into the front window. I heard my mother yelling, and the bus driver was saying, "What happened? What happened?" as I literally ripped open the front door and started running along Hylan Boulevard. I ran and ran and I could hardly see from the flashing lights on some of the stores. There were some kids yelling things and a lot of traffic and cars pulling in and out of a McDonald's, but I finally reached New Dorp Lane and headed up toward the railroad station. All I could think about was getting a train. It'd let me off above the town of Oakwood Kills, but if I ran I'd get back quicker than waiting for the bus. I kept running and then I thought of hitchhiking and started running with my thumb out but I didn't look where I was going so I ran into a mailbox. All I could see was this vision of Lloyd Dipardi climbing the attic stairs to see if we'd left anything and when he saw my father's coat he'd take a knife and mutilate it in some awful original way. There would be this basket of cloth shreds waiting for me on the front steps. Then I saw a red neon sign that said TAXI. I barged into the office and told the dispatcher I wanted a cab to Oakwood Kills. He was wearing a neck brace and told me to hold my horses. I had to wait about five minutes before this old Chevy pulled out with FLASH COM-MUTER SERVICE stenciled on it. I jumped in and told the driver I wanted 16 Half Moon Street on the double. I didn't care if it took my last dime. As the taxi cruised along my thoughts were jumping from one thing to another. It was like I was dreaming but I was wide awake. I began to remember the most obscure things like I was trapped in a time machine or something. I remembered when I was a kid and used to want to be Superboy and tie a cape around my neck and leap off roofs to catch lawbreakers and battle evil forces—following which I would be rewarded by a roller-skating date with the pert heroine of my choice. And I remembered my major social success was when I was seven and lived in Travis and gave ghost shows. I invited all the kids on the block to come into a shack one by one and I shook hands with them in the dark wearing a rubber glove with cold cream on it. I was popular for a whole week in that neighborhood. I had a whole lot of other thoughts, too. Even as a toddler I thought my goals were in line with basic human values. I used to save centipedes from being de-legged by other children. I used to untie tin cans from cats' tails and a lot of other kids just hated me for it. But I guess in the long run I was a freak. After all, what other kid on earth would have spent as much time as I did growing up and yearning with all his heart that just one morning he could wake up and find his father at the breakfast table.

16

THE CAB STOPPED IN FRONT OF LLOYD'S HOUSE AND I GOT
out. I think the driver thought I was going to run
away without paying but my slacks were so tight I
couldn't get my money out of my pocket without
standing up. I gave him the fare, including a good tip,
which left me with about a dollar and twenty-nine
cents to my name. It was the absolute end of my savings from the last case my mother had, where her boss
gave me a couple of dollars a day to walk his Yorkies.
The driver just floored his junk heap and took off
making so much noise I didn't hear the lilt of music
until the taxi turned at the far corner. It had been
quite a while since Helen and I had vacated the place
and I couldn't believe the party was still going on. The
song playing was one of Lloyd's oldies with some male
group singing "Let's Do It."

The lyrics went something like "Birds do it, Bees do

it"—and it was a real catchy tune but not the kind
of thing any modern kid would dance to. Anyway,
now we're getting to the part of this confession that's
going to be the hardest for me to tell you about. I became immediately aware that the house was absolutely silent except for the low music playing, and the
lyrics were very funny but I wasn't laughing. They
were now something about "Sponges do it, Oysters do
it, Let's fall in love," like I said.

There was only a dim light coming from inside the
house, but it was enough for me to see that the living
room and kitchen were empty. I had the distinct feeling the party *was* over.

I went into the kitchen where the long and short of
it was that the house had been ransacked. Now,
granted, it's difficult to tell when a house which looked
like a cataclysm to begin with has been ransacked,
but this place had been ravaged. The most obvious
loss was revealed by the wide-open doors of the tallboy showing that all the bottles of Wild Turkey had
flown the coop. The vodka, gin, and chartreuse were
all gone. I looked in the refrigerator and that seemed
pretty empty except for a bottle of horseradish and
some Dijon mustard. In other parlance, this joint was
wiped out, including the living-room speakers. Well,
I had come back for my father's coat, I told myself, so
I just headed straight for the attic steps, but I was so
disturbed about what might be happening to Carmelita I couldn't help but look in on her.

The door to Lloyd's bedroom was open. Carmelita
was still lying there looking unconscious, but I could
see she was still breathing and the oxygen was flowing

correctly. Sitting in the big stuffed chair near the bottom of the bed was Lloyd and he looked very depressed. He didn't even look up to see it was me in the doorway. He just kept staring at Carmelita. Just then the record finished and the arm of the turntable swung back, made a click, and then automatically started the record over again. "Birds do it, Bees do it! . . ."

Well, I figured now I'd better go right up to the attic, so I went quietly out to the hall. I had the vision of Dad's coat hanging on the rafter near the window—and I was just about to go up the stairs when I stopped because I heard voices. I listened and I knew they weren't coming from Lloyd's room. I went down a couple more steps thinking it was probably just the old man watching television—but then I realized one of the voices sounded like Rosemary's. Then I saw this couple in the shadows of the room at the end of the hall—the room where Carmelita had first been installed.

"Rosemary?" I whispered, starting down the hall. "Rosemary, *is that you?*"

I felt my way along the wall of the hallway until I reached the room. I found the light switch and flicked it on. There were Rosemary and Apollo staring at me like two guilty moths. To say that they looked disheveled would be an understatement. Dolly had certainly been right. I wasn't Rosemary's type. Rosemary's type was the handsome and strong kind of kid who looked like he had everything.

"How's the party going?" Apollo asked. He was loaded and I just ignored his question.

143

"Rosemary, I was looking for you all night. I was worried about you."

"There's no reason to worry about her when she's in good hands," Apollo dribbled.

"I'm not so sure about that," I said.

"We're just talking in here," Rosemary said.

"Now why don't you just beat it?" Apollo asked.

I wasn't going to be humiliated and I wasn't going to leave that room before I spoke to Rosemary.

"May I talk with you?" I requested politely of her.

"Sure," she said, squinting her eyes and straightening her clothes. "But the light hurts my eyes," she added, snapping down the switch. There was still enough illumination from the moonlight bouncing through the open window to see her clearly enough.

"I mean alone," I clarified.

"All right," Rosemary agreed.

"Make it fast," Apollo grunted.

Rosemary followed me out of the room into the hallway. "I thought you liked *me*," I said, barely able to speak.

"I do."

"Then why were you with *him?*"

"I like him, too," she smiled.

"But you like *me*."

"Can't I like more than one person at the same time?" she asked.

"No," I said weakly.

"Why can't I?" she asked innocently.

"If you like him, you couldn't like me," I said, and I felt so terrible I turned my back on her and started down the hall.

Rosemary called after me, "Chris, please don't leave. Let's talk."

"Forget it," I called back. "There's nothing to talk about. You're just not the girl I thought you were."

I stopped at the end of the hall and turned to see Apollo come out and put his arm around her. One thing I knew for sure was that I needed a beer so I went out to the kitchen and really looked in the refrigerator. I finally found a couple of Schaefers that had survived the fete by rolling to the back of a bottom shelf behind some old vegetables. I opened one and it sprayed all over me but I didn't even squint, that's how numb I was, as Apollo and Rosemary walked right by me. For a moment it seemed she was going to say something but Apollo just grunted and practically yanked her out of the house. The screen door slammed and I just figured, *Chris, ol' boy, you are now at what is poetically referred to as your nadir. El bottom. La gutter. Finis. Kaput.*

Finally, I found the energy to carry me and my beer to Lloyd's open bedroom door. I leaned against one side and after a minute or so Lloyd turned his head to look at me.

"I guess I'm everything you said I was," I mumbled and took a big sip of my beer.

Lloyd turned his gaze back to Carmelita. He didn't say a word. He just kept his eyes on his mother. I shifted my weight and leaned against the other side of the doorway while Lloyd reached to the left of his chair and brought a bottle of Wild Turkey up to his lips.

"You don't have to be a loser," he said from the depths of his stupor.

Suddenly a shiver ran through me because of a change in the expression on Carmelita's face. Her eyes had opened a slit and were looking at me.

"I'm afraid," she said with a look very much like the look she had given me in the ambulance when I first met her. Then she closed her eyes. I went over to Lloyd and whispered, "We'd better call the doctor." He responded as though he hadn't heard a word I said.

"In Italy some fathers take their sons to a whorehouse for their thirteenth-birthday present," Lloyd said solemnly, almost helplessly, as he continued staring at his mother.

I realized then that Lloyd was going to be of absolutely no help with Carmelita, so I hurried to the phone on the table next to Lloyd. The piece of paper Helen had left with the doctor's number was missing. "Where's the doctor's phone number?" I yelled. Lloyd turned his head to look at me and I knew he didn't know what I was talking about. I grabbed up the receiver and dialed Information.

"I need the number for Ewing Hospital in Manhattan," I sputtered frantically.

"Just one moment," the operator said.

"It's an emergency!" I pleaded.

"Do you want the main number or visiting-hour information?" the stupid operator asked.

"The main number!"

"The main number is 555-0866," the operator said. I disconnected instantly and dialed the number. As it was ringing Carmelita's head moved upward slightly and then fell backward onto the pillow. The phone was still ringing as I reached over to take Carmelita's wrist in my hand. My fingers searched for a pulse but there was none. I tried to find the slightest sign of life for at least five minutes and still no one was answering the phone. I hung up because I knew it didn't matter if anyone answered now.

"She's dead," I said quietly.

Lloyd was watching me now and I could tell his mind had shut out everything else in the room. It was as if he hadn't understood me, but I knew he did.

"There may not be a happy ending for her and me," he said, managing to get up out of the chair. He moved closer to Carmelita as if pulled by an invisible hand. "But there could be one for you." He reached out his hand and gently stroked her sleeve. "I'm sorry, Mom, I didn't want you to die," he said. His words came slower and slower and I frankly got the feeling I was in a room with two corpses. I felt my knees begin to go weak but I fought to hold myself upright until I could make it into the living room. I just sank down onto the rug and at that moment I couldn't think of a single thing to move for. It was as though every cell in my body just wanted to be left alone. It was like a complete surrender. I didn't close my eyes. I just lay on my stomach looking at how strange the kitchen table and chairs looked from my position on the living-room rug. They seemed to loom up like great chrome poles and I didn't have the strength to lift my eyes high enough to see where they ended. A moment later there was another body lying next to me on the floor. I felt Lloyd's arm reach across my shoulder and hold on to me.

147

"Don't let them keep you afraid," he slurred.

I didn't know whether I was coming or going and all he did was hold me tighter. I knew the fact that his mother was dead was getting through to him. "It's not too late for you. Don't let anyone stop you from having what you deserve," he whispered in my ear.

Well, I must confess I didn't know whether I understood Lloyd so much as I did understand that some people had come in through the screen door. Just the amount of creaking in the bungalow floor told me there was more than one person and whoever they were they had come to a halt in the kitchen. With just a little effort I focused my eyes and recognized one pair of feet in white shoes as belonging to my mother and there were six other legs behind her which I could tell by the deep blue color of the uniforms belonged to what is known on this globe as cops.

17

IF THERE'S ONE THING THAT REALLY MAKES YOU SNAP TO it's the sight of your mother flanked by three guys wearing guns. In a flash Helen was pulling me up off the floor.

"Did he do anything to you?" she asked.

"No," I said, rubbing my eyes. She started talking a mile a minute, but those cops hardly said a word. They moved around like they had been in rehearsal for this scene for about thirty years. Two of the cops looked like disgruntled orangutans and the third looked sort of like Goliath. They were all what you'd call on the chunky side and they walked like it had been their first time out of their squad cars in weeks.

"We want a little talk with you, Mr. Dipardi," one of the cops said paternally as they lifted Lloyd to his feet and led him into the bedroom. For a while I was so mixed up I could hardly speak. My mother was screaming and the cops were using some kind of divide-and-conquer technique. They found Carmelita's body and asked my mother to check her out to make certain she was deceased, while the Goliath cop cornered me in the kitchen and kept asking, "What did he do, kid? Come on, you can trust me. Don't be afraid."

"He didn't do anything," I said. I must have said that a dozen times, but it didn't seem to do any good. The cops all kept their voices under perfect control and moved like machines back and forth through the house. I could see there were two police cars in front of the house and I just thought the whole thing seemed a little unfair the way the cops were firing questions at poor Lloyd. He was straining to answer, and they kept him out of my sight while they played this shuffle routine. Two of the cops were really working on me at one point saying things like: "Did he do the same thing to you as he did to the other kids? Trust us. Nobody's going to get hurt, just trust us and we'll see Mr. Dipardi gets the help he needs."

My mother came storming out of the bedroom and she seemed to do nothing but keep saying, "I want that drunk locked up! You already know what he did with the other kid." At that I realized the cops had already paid a call at Harold's house thanks to Helen.

"Lloyd didn't do anything," I swore again.

"You shut up," Helen said. "Harold told all they need to lock him up and throw away the key."

I could tell by her face that Harold really had spilled the beans. If there was one thing I could have suspected the moment I first met Harold was that he wouldn't be able to hold his own in a cross-examination, particularly if he was as hurt as he looked when Lloyd slapped him.

"You wait here," Goliath said, leading me out onto the porch. I was sort of just spinning around not knowing what to say or do. I wondered why the cops wanted me on the porch but then I realized they were pulling a number on Helen. They began by trying to calm her down. The cops let her sound off, but slowly and calculatedly, they began to slip her little facts. *"You're one hundred percent right,"* and *"We understand exactly how you feel."* Finally, they were saying things like *"The shame of it is he'll be out on bail in a day. They let them get away with anything nowadays. You take them in and they get a lawyer and they're right back out on the street. It gets in the papers. If you press charges your name gets in too."* Then there was a bit of whispering that I couldn't hear and finally two of the cops went into the bedroom, and Goliath took Helen and me outside and down the driveway. "You wait a few minutes in the patrol car and officers Collins and Burns will give you a lift."

"Where are my suitcases?" Helen asked, looking a bit dusty from the whole experience.

"They're still in the front car," he assured her, showing the way. "Where will you be going?"

"The Ritz Hotel," Helen said.

"The officers'll drop you off. You just forget the whole thing ever happened and we won't be wasting any of the taxpayers' money," he added with a strange inflection in his voice. It was as though he had struck

151

up some kind of deal with Helen. "Do you like to play basketball?" he asked me as though it was a logical progression of thought and in such a patronizing way I could tell he was trying to distract my attention from the house—like he was worried I'd hear something I shouldn't.

"No," I said, my ears straining to listen.

"What you need is the PAL or a Big Brother," he advised, squeezing my shoulder. *"If you were my kid you'd be playing football."*

"If I were your kid I'd be playing horse," I said.

"Horse?" he asked, looking a little puzzled as he opened the patrol-car door.

"You know," I clarified, "I'd be the front end—and you could just be yourself."

Suddenly, I heard sounds from the house. I had one foot into the car when I realized they were muffled cries of pain mixed with what sounded like repeated *thuds*. Before the cop or Helen could stop me I scooted back up the driveway. I bounded up the porch steps, practically ripped the screen door off its hinges, and rushed into the house. I ran to the hallway where I saw the cops beating Lloyd, pounding their fists into his ribs. I went berserk at the sight and rushed in, kicking and punching the cops with all my might. I grabbed one of the cops around the neck and he swung me off the ground. I began screaming ridiculous things like *"He got rid of the kid's nits! He taught him to be clean! He taught him how to eat! He didn't eat right!"* I just kept punching and I knew they didn't know or care what on earth I was talking about. Finally they threw me backward and before

I knew what had happened I was being carried out of the house by Goliath. I hadn't even noticed him zipping up from behind and I was still swinging and kicking, but all I seemed to hit was the air. I was still screaming *"Don't beat him anymore!"* when reflexively I rammed my knee forward and connected with something. The cop let go and went stumbling backward and I then fled through approximately sixteen back yards until I was halted by a rather large rosebush thicket about two blocks behind Lloyd's house. For the moment I had escaped.

18

IT TOOK ME A GOOD HALF HOUR TO CIRCLE THE NEIGH-
borhood and get into a good hiding position behind a
large blue spruce tree across the street from Lloyd's
house. Both cop cars were still in front and my mother
was leaning against the first one talking to Goliath
while they all were looking up and down the street. I
figured by now they had to face the fact that I was
gone and the only logical place I'd eventually turn up
would be the Ritz Hotel. After a few minutes the cor-
oner's van arrived and they took Carmelita's body out
and drove away with it.

About ten minutes later Officers Collins and Burns
came out of the house and strutted down the driveway. They stood and talked with Helen and Goliath
for a couple of minutes and I could tell they were
talking about me the way they were gawking up and
down the street. Finally, they just opened the door of

the first patrol car and Helen got in. Officers Collins and Burns got in the front and they drove off leaving Goliath behind. I saw my mother's profile as the car pulled away and I might as well confess that half of me was glad she was heading for the Ritz, but the other half hoped she was crying or worried over me.

Goliath got into his squad car and I figured he was just going to drive away. Instead he just sat and waited about five minutes and I was puzzled when he started the engine, backed up the car, and then pulled into Lloyd's driveway. He drove all the way up close to the garage, put out the lights and shut off the engine. I heard the door of his car open and close. A few seconds after that there was the sound of the screen door making its usual slam. I figured maybe he had forgotten something.

I waited about twenty minutes before my curiosity got the best of me. Then I left the security of the blue spruce and went around the entire block to approach Lloyd's house through the back yard. Maybe Goliath was drowning Lloyd in the pool or something. Perhaps that was the latest thing in jurisprudence. Whatever, I knew I would never be able to leave without knowing that Lloyd was okay. I finally got up enough guts to go up to the rear of the house and as far as I could tell there was still only the one light on and that was the one in Lloyd's bedroom. It took me only three minutes to decide on a plan of action because I noticed the window in the back room of the house was open. I reached up and without making any noise I pulled myself up and over the sill. Once inside I sat on the floor in darkness until I got my bearings. The rented hospital bed and cot were easy enough to see from the moonlight, but I mainly kept my ears cocked for any sound of approaching feet. My ventricles finally quieted down enough so I could hear the faint sounds of a television playing in old Mr. Dipardi's room. Slowly, I opened the door of the back room and looked down the hall. There was only a slice of light spilling out of the half-open door of Lloyd's bedroom.

I heard voices coming from Lloyd's room as I started down the hall and I was sorry the bathroom door in the hall was closed because maybe I could have seen something without having to risk getting too close to the bedroom. Somehow in all my worrying about Lloyd I had totally forgotten about the stairway leading up to the attic—and my father's coat. I never thought anything in the world would make me forget that coat again. I then also remembered the crack in the attic floor! *The crack!* I started up the stairs as though I was walking on steps made of balloons. It must have taken me a good five minutes to lift up the floorboards and insulation without making a sound. I did the whole procedure as though I was de-fusing a bomb and at last I lay on the floor and lowered my right eye to the slit.

Lloyd was lying on the bed, and he had a couple of Band-Aids on his face. He wasn't moaning or anything and I was thankful he was still alive. The stuffed chair had been moved over near the bathroom door and Goliath was sitting in it smoking a cigarette like he was visiting a sick friend. It all seemed very social, and he was telling Lloyd stuff like I'm going to tell you now but maybe not in the exact order in which he said it.

"My two buddies want a thousand each. I want two thousand. If I make the parties concerned press charges you'll need a lawyer like Reiger or Brassman and the judge would want something like five or six thousand dollars under the table to give a suspended sentence."

I couldn't tell from Lloyd's eyes exactly what he was thinking or feeling. The only thing I could see was something of the kind of look he had had on his face when Helen and the attendants had brought in Carmelita, and he had said, "Hi, Mom. It's good to have you home"—which had been the only real moment I had glimpsed that somewhere inside of him he must have loved his mother very much but the wires had gotten crossed. I guess that expression of affection can end up limited when your mother comes after you with a lighted match when you're three years old.

Goliath continued, "If my buddies and I get paid off it won't be in the newspapers. You'll keep your job." Goliath paused and took a puff on his cigarette.

Lloyd lifted his head and put his hands behind his neck. All he did was nod. At least from my position it looked like a nod. There was some more talk about money and payoffs and the cop said, "I know a couple of other guys like you." He picked himself up from the chair. Heading toward the door he added, "It must be lonely being the way you are." Then the cop left the room. The screen door slammed, and a minute later I heard the police car start up and drive off.

Lloyd leaned over and put a record on the turntable. Then he lay motionless on the bed before the arm of the stereo touched the record. A quartet started singing some extra-old-fashioned song. It went something like "Come! Come! I love you only, My heart is true." Lloyd lay as still as if he was frozen, and now that I knew he was safe from being beaten anymore I breathed a sigh of relief. But then, I started hearing strange sounds. This time the sounds were in my own head. They were the sounds of my mind like the whisper of tears falling. And they were the sounds of kids calling me CRY-BABY ROOSTER HEAD! There were the sounds of so many of the characters from the past and present melting together to form one giant villain. Of Officers Collins and Burns and Goliath and Helen and Apollo, and Carmelita lunging forward to bite me. It was the collective sounds of everyone who had ever rejected or hurt me —a huge fanged persecutor forming in the darkness of the attic room and pressing my eye so tightly to the crack that a slender ray of light seemed to join me with the man on the bed below. I could see tears rolling out of Lloyd's eyes now and I began to cry with him because I realized if it hadn't been for the things he had told me—no, not *told* me: screamed at me, blared at me, *stalked* me with—maybe I would have ended up being like him.

Lloyd reached out a hand to the stereo dials and slowly the volume grew louder and louder. "Come! Come! I love you only." He turned it up so loud I began to feel the vibrations from the speakers sock the bedroom ceiling and seep upward into the attic floor and into my stomach, when suddenly Lloyd sat up and swung his legs over the edge of the bed. What he did then was so fast it seemed to be over before I could move. He grabbed a pistol from under his mattress and before I could cry out he was back on the bed with the barrel of the gun pointed at his head. "Come! Come! I love you only" shrieked out of the speakers and with what seemed a single motion Lloyd put a pillow over his head and there was a shot. I pulled away from the crack so fast I hit my head on the bed so hard I don't remember too clearly what happened after that. I ran down those attic stairs like they were on fire. I raced into Lloyd's bedroom with the music still exploding out of the speakers and all I remember is poor Lloyd on the bed. I just stood there, shaking, and the singing kept coming—"Come! Come! Naught can efface you"—and I felt so lost and helpless and like I wanted to talk to Lloyd but I knew nobody would ever be talking to him again. Just take my word for it because I don't want to describe what I saw. I just turned away and walked out of the house in a daze.

19

I WALKED DOWN THE STREET JUST LIKE I HAD DONE THAT evening when Harold and I went to the movies, but this time I felt more alone than ever in my life. Even the moon couldn't comfort me as I started walking toward it. I had nowhere special to go. I knew I would have to call the police and tell them if for nobody else's sake than for poor old Mr. Dipardi's who was probably still obliviously watching TV. I passed a big willow tree. A white picket fence. A few streetlights. The chilly air made my nose run. I started wiping it with my sleeve, when I remembered I had a tissue in my pocket. Good old Lloyd. He would have had something to say about a kid who wiped his nose on his sleeve. I gave my nose a good blow. Then I could smell the night air and it seemed to revive me so I took a deep breath and felt the evening dew go down deep into my lungs. It felt so good I did it again. And again. And again. Then I looked up at a signpost and it still said Half Moon Street.

I walked about a block farther when I thought I saw a figure sitting down at the next corner on a bus-stop bench. I figured the moon was playing tricks because it was too late for anybody to be out, no less waiting on a bus bench. Actually, I couldn't tell for sure if it was a person or a garbage bag or something. I walked toward the bench, not hearing a sound except a few crickets who seemed like they had decided to take a night walk with me. It took my mind off things trying to determine whether they were having a conversation through their chirps or if all their noises were just meaningless, useless. After I came to no conclusion at all, I saw the thing on the bench near the curb and it was definitely not a bag. As a matter of fact, I could tell it was distinctly human. It looked like a girl, and as I got closer I was surprised to see it was Rosemary. She didn't notice me at first, I could tell—but finally she heard my footsteps approaching and she turned around.

"Rosemary," I said, "what are you doing here?"

"I'm thinking," she answered clearly, even though her eyes looked like she had been crying. I could also tell she was happy to see me again because her pupils widened up just a bit. I hated to tell her but I figured I'd better get it over with quick. "Lloyd shot himself," I said.

For a moment I thought she hadn't heard me. Then she turned her gaze to the ground and asked in a voice I could barely hear, "Is he dead?"

"Yes," I said, and I was determined to let it go at

that as I sat on the bench next to her. She didn't look like she could handle anything about Carmelita or the cops or any of that. She just seemed to know better than to draw me out so we both didn't say anything for a very long time. Finally she spoke in a low voice.

"Tonight, Lloyd and I were talking in the bedroom," she started. "I tried telling him all the things he had to live for, all the good things that he did for kids and how we really needed him and liked him, but he was so depressed he wouldn't believe me. He yelled at me and told me to keep my mouth shut." Her voice broke off.

"Why are you sitting here?" I asked. "You'll get sick. It's cold."

"I'm not very smart," she said softly, and I knew she was referring to Apollo. God only knows what had happened and he probably had ended up ditching her.

We sat a few more minutes in silence alone with each other and the crickets.

"Rosemary," I finally said, "now that I'm ready to learn, he's not here anymore." She didn't answer and I wasn't really expecting her to.

The moon shone down on us and my eyes followed the rays up into the sky.

I looked at the moon for a very long time and remembered it was the same moon that just hours before had shone down on Lloyd when he had stood on his car roof at the boatyard in all his majestic agony and told me about how to be a man. And now, it was the very same moon shining on Rosemary and me. Rosemary followed my gaze and we watched the moon move behind a small cloud and start its journey back out until its other half became visible. It seemed to be suspended in time and space, and at that moment I had the strangest thought: The moon was playing tricks, casting only half a shadow. I suddenly realized that what seemed like an illusion was really true. I was only half a shadow and only half of what I could be. And it was at this instant something momentous happened to me. I remembered I had left my father's coat behind but this time it didn't matter. I felt as though I was unfolding under the moonlight. I was opening up like a seed that had been thrust painfully and deeply—even ruthlessly—into the ground and given a merciless warning and command to grow. The cloud that had been hanging over me for so many years of my life on earth was suddenly lifting thanks to an anguished, tormented man who now lay lifeless on a bed not far away. And when the moon moved again from behind the cloud it seemed I felt an understanding and a compassion for the entire human race. Especially for Lloyd, for Rosemary, for Helen, for my father who had run away—and even for the Apollo who seemed to have everything. Even for a full moon there is always its dark side which can never be seen, which can never be fully known, and which will always be the mystery that is called Life. And I was ready to accept that, and yet for some reason I was most interested in the things in my life I *could* change. The things I could see if I tried hard enough. The things *I deserved*, as Lloyd had told me.

I reached out and took Rosemary's hand in mine and we sat there a long, long time. Then after a while, I began to look past the moon, past all the great satellites of Jupiter, and dream upon the stars.

ABOUT THE AUTHOR

PAUL ZINDEL has established himself as an outstanding playwright and novelist. He was born on Staten Island and now lives in Connecticut. He is the author of *The Effect of Gamma Rays on Man-in-the-Moon Marigolds*, which won the 1971 Pulitzer Prize for Drama and the New York Critics Circle Award. His first two novels, *The Pigman* and *My Darling, My Hamburger*, were selected as Outstanding Books of the Year by *The New York Times*. Mr. Zindel is also the author of *I Never Loved Your Mind* and, most recently, *Confessions of a Teenage Baboon*. His other plays include *And Miss Reardon Drinks a Little*, *Let Me Hear You Whisper* and *The Secret Affairs of Mildred Wild*.

VOICES OF PAUL ZINDEL

"I love the school cafeteria in fifth period because there's a girl in there with long, straight, black hair, whose name is Edna Shinglebox, and she looks as freaky and depressed as I am."

Marsh Mellow in PARDON ME, YOU'RE STEPPING ON MY EYEBALL!

"Since lunch I went to the gym and cut 7th period. I'm sending you this via Helen Mackey if she goes to your 9th. Just had to tell you they started doing wheelbarrows in gym. I refused! I told the looney teacher I was under the care of a chiropractor and he said wheelbarrows weren't good for me. Have you seen Sean? He hasn't called me all week. I don't care. If you see him, make sure you tell him I don't care."

Liz Carstensen's note in MY DARLING, MY HAMBURGER

"I don't really know what I'm going to do. It's not going to be that Love Land crap. And I'm not going to give civilization a kick in the behind, because I might need an appendectomy sometime. But I'm going to do something, and I have a strange feeling it's going to be phantasmagorically different."

Dewey Daniels in I NEVER LOVED YOUR MIND

"My name is Christopher. My friends would call me Chris, but I don't have any friends. No real friends. I also have no father. Now, once upon a time I did have a father and my father and Helen really loved each other very much for the first seven years they were married, and then after that they hated each other so much that my father pulled that old trick of saying he was going out to buy the evening paper but went to Mexico."

Christopher Boyd in CONFESSIONS OF A TEENAGE BABOON

These are a few of the many voices created by Paul Zindel in his popular novels that have become worldwide favorites. In addition to the above books, his successful works include THE PIGMAN and the Pulitzer Prize-winning play, THE EFFECT OF GAMMA RAYS ON MAN-IN-THE-MOON MARIGOLDS. His stories are about loners, with bad complexions, goofy parents and startling problems.

Zindel's books reflect teenage living—both the joys and the pains. As he says, "Teenagers feel they are misfits. They're at an age when they *should* feel out of place. It's a natural condition. I know it's a continuing battle to get through the years between twelve and twenty, so I always write from the teenager's point of view."

Zindel's own early years were difficult. Besides using those experiences, he bases his plots and characters on what he learned listening to student problems in the years he taught high school chemistry.

When he quit teaching Paul Zindel began to put all his observations and insights to work and started writing. The result has been a series of zany novels which are reaching an ever-growing audience of teenagers.

Zindel lives in Manhattan with his wife and two children. His latest book, THE UNDERTAKER'S GONE BANANAS, has just been published in hardcover by Harper & Row.

Meet Paul Zindel in all the books published by Bantam Books. Now available wherever paperbacks are sold.

TEENAGERS FACE LIFE AND LOVE

oose books filled with fun and adventure, discovery
d disenchantment, failure and conquest, triumph and
gedy, life and love.

13359	**THE LATE GREAT ME** Sandra Scoppettone	$1.95
13691	**HOME BEFORE DARK** Sue Ellen Bridgers	$1.75
13671	**ALL TOGETHER NOW** Sue Ellen Bridgers	$1.95
12501	**PARDON ME, YOU'RE STEPPING ON MY EYEBALL!** Paul Zindel	$1.95
11091	**A HOUSE FOR JONNIE O.** Blossom Elfman	$1.95
14306	**ONE FAT SUMMER** Robert Lipsyte	$1.95
13184	**I KNOW WHY THE CAGED BIRD SINGS** Maya Angelou	$2.25
12650	**QUEEN OF HEARTS** Bill & Vera Cleaver	$1.75
12741	**MY DARLING, MY HAMBURGER** Paul Zindel	$1.95
13555	**HEY DOLLFACE** Deborah Hautzig	$1.75
13897	**WHERE THE RED FERN GROWS** Wilson Rawls	$2.25
11829	**CONFESSIONS OF A TEENAGE BABOON** Paul Zindel	$1.95
11838	**OUT OF LOVE** Hilma Wolitzer	$1.50
13352	**SOMETHING FOR JOEY** Richard E. Peck	$1.95
13440	**SUMMER OF MY GERMAN SOLDIER** Bette Greene	$1.95
13693	**WINNING** Robin Brancato	$1.95
13628	**IT'S NOT THE END OF THE WORLD** Judy Blume	$1.95

uy them at your local bookstore or use this handy coupon for ordering:

Bantam Book Catalog

Here's your up-to-the-minute listing of over 1,400 titles by your favorite authors.

This illustrated, large format catalog gives a description of each title. For your convenience, it is divided into categories in fiction and non-fiction—gothics, science fiction, westerns, mysteries, cookbooks, mysticism and occult, biographies, history, family living, health, psychology, art.

So don't delay—take advantage of this special opportunity to increase your reading pleasure.

Just send us your name and address and 50¢ (to help defray postage and handling costs).